Honeysuckle Lovelace

The Dog Walkers' Club

Cherry Whytock

Honeysuckle Lovelace

The Dog Walkers' Club

PICCADILLY PRESS · LONDON

For Olive and the puppies

First published in Great Britain in 2006
by Piccadilly Press Ltd.,
5 Castle Road, London NW1 8PR
www.piccadillypress.co.uk

A catalogue record for this book is available from the British Library

ISBN: 1 85340 889 1 (trade paperback)
EAN: 9 781853 408892

1 3 5 7 9 10 8 6 4 2

Printed and bound in Great Britain by Bookmarque Ltd
Cover design and text design by Simon Davis
Typeset by M Rules, London

Set in 12 Adobe Caslon

Chapter One

'You know there are some insane people in the world who think living like this is romantic!' said Rita as she tripped over the edge of the zebra-striped cupboard while trying to pull on her purple fishnet tights. 'But I can tell them, it blinking well isn't!'

Honeysuckle Lovelace leaned against the fridge in their tiny galley kitchen and munched her Frosties. There was no point arguing with her mum or pointing out that she knew perfectly well that living on a houseboat was way more exciting than living in a high-rise flat. Rita was always cranky in the morning. She needed to put on her earrings and stick on fresh nicotine patches before she could be nice to anyone. Giving up smoking was one of Rita's main aims in life, but it was making her quite short-tempered.

'Shall I make you some coffee?' asked Honeysuckle.

'And, of course,' continued Rita, ignoring her, 'today has to be Saturday, doesn't it? The day when most sensible people stay under their bedclothes until at least midday . . . but not me! Oh no! I have to get myself all dolled up and totter down to the salon to primp and perm the likes of Mrs Whitely-Grub so that I can afford to stop this . . . this floating disaster from sinking!'

Rita struggled into her green Doc Marten boots and straightened her rainbow-striped tank top. Her hair was bright, shocking red that week and it was standing up in little tufts all round her head. She clipped on her favourite, chandelier-style diamanté earrings, rolled up her sleeve, stuck on her nicotine patches and took up a *Hello!* magazine-style pose. 'How do I look?' she asked.

'Great!' said Honeysuckle handing her mum a rosy-printed mug full of steaming hot black coffee. Rita flopped dramatically on to the faded green velvet bunk before taking the mug and gulping down the coffee.

'So, what are you up to today?'

'Oh, nothing much,' said Honeysuckle. 'Just hanging out – I might come into the salon later and see how Mrs Whitely-Grub's blue rinse is going!'

Rita snorted. 'D'you know what? I think I'll do it pink today for a change! Or purple with orange spots. That would surprise the old biddy!'

Honeysuckle giggled.

'Oh,' said Rita, drumming her fingers on the colourful cushion next to her. 'I'm gasping for a ciggie – do you think one little one before work would matter?'

'Yes, it would, definitely,' replied Honeysuckle. 'Try sucking that pretend cigarette thing again – that usually works, doesn't it?'

Rita reached for the white plastic tube that was supposed to look like a cigarette and dragged furiously on it. 'Aargh! It's hopeless,' she said chucking it back in its box. 'I think I need a doughnut instead. Are there any left in the packet?'

Honeysuckle handed her the last remaining doughnut, which Rita began to jam into her mouth. 'I'll be the size of a house at this rate,' she said when her mouth was less jammed. 'I mean, which is worse? Fags or flab?'

'Fags,' said Honeysuckle, 'and anyway you'll never get fat, you don't keep still long enough to get fat!'

'Here, Honeybunch – you have the rest,' said Rita tossing Honeysuckle the half-eaten doughnut. 'I've got to go – off into the world of wet hair and curlers. Be amazingly good, won't you and make sure everything's shipshape if you go out.'

'Aye aye, Captain!' said Honeysuckle saluting her. Rita disappeared up the tiny stairs to the hatch that opened above the end of Honeysuckle's bunk. The exchange was a morning ritual – a sort of good luck charm, something they had to say to each other to make the day go right.

When Rita had vanished like a miniature whirlwind off in the direction of the high street and her hairdressing salon, Curl Up and Dye, Honeysuckle hummed a bit of 'Dancing Queen' and looked round the brightly painted saloon.

She loved this 'floating disaster' as Rita called it. The little wood-burning stove made the tiny space as warm as toast and there were shimmering silvery shadows across the walls where the early morning October sun reflected off the water. Rita was right – lots of people did think it was romantic to live on a houseboat, but Honeysuckle didn't really know whether it was romantic or not. All right, it was exciting when the rain poured down and thundered about on the roof of The Patchwork Snail before rushing down in torrents into the surrounding canal. And it was beautiful to see the stars reflected in the water at night and comforting to hear the lap, lap of the ripples against the sides of the boat when you were trying to get to sleep. But it could also be scary and annoying if a big swanky boat came past too fast and made your floating home bounce about so much that your bowl of Frosties landed up in your lap. Mostly though, The Patchwork Snail just felt like home – the place Honeysuckle and her mum had lived for ever and ever.

Honeysuckle squeezed herself into the world's smallest bathroom (painted with mermaids and weird-coloured fish by Rita and Honeysuckle in an effort to disguise the mould that insisted on growing on the walls) and looked at herself in the mirror. She thought for the millionth time that she really didn't look much like her mum. Only her nose was the same: small and slightly turned up at the end. But her heart-shaped face, her tonne and a half of black curly hair and her pale blue eyes were nothing like Rita's. Although, as far as she could remember, she had never seen him, Honeysuckle knew that she looked like her dad. And she also knew that because of him, somewhere in her background she had real Romany ancestors.

Lenny, Honeysuckle's dad, disappeared when Honeysuckle was a baby. According to Rita he went on a gap year and owing to the gap between his ears where his brain should have been, he forgot to come home. Honeysuckle didn't miss him – why would she? She didn't remember anything about him. There were just two things that she knew about Lenny: one was that he left her a crystal ball, and the other was that her dark hair and exotic looks weren't the only things she had inherited from her dad – Honeysuckle Sabrina Florette Lovelace was absolutely convinced that she had fortune-telling powers.

While she finished washing she sang '– *You can dance, you can ji–ive, having the time of your li–i–ife . . .*' loudly. When Honeysuckle was a baby Rita had sung her Abba songs to lull her to sleep and ever since, she had loved Abba more than any other band in the whole world. Then Honeysuckle put on her favourite patched velvet jeans, black polo neck jumper (with silver crochet flowers added by Honeysuckle herself), pushed on twenty-seven multi-coloured bangles, threaded some of last Christmas's tinsel through her hair, and set about making herself a cup of tea.

Every morning she did the same thing: she put the green enamel kettle on the little stove and found the rosy teapot. She never, ever made tea with teabags. What would be the point? If you made tea with teabags there were no tea-leaves left in the bottom of your cup and without tea-leaves in the bottom of your cup, how could you tell what your fortune for the day would be? Even people without real Romany in their blood knew that the pictures and patterns that the tea-leaves made when you had drunk your tea could be read (by a very talented fortune teller) to tell you what the day would hold in store. So each morning Honeysuckle drank her tea and then set about 'reading the signs'.

On this particular morning, when Honeysuckle had swished the remains of her tea around in the cup, turned the cup upside down on to the saucer, and then turned it right-side up again, the remaining tea-leaves looked like nothing but a splodge with four bits sticking out. But hang on! When Honeysuckle turned the cup around, so that the handle was pointing away from her, there quite clearly was a picture of a dog! Why on earth would the tea-leaves show a picture of a dog? Honeysuckle hadn't got a dog, much as she would have loved one.

Not being able to have a pet was one of the bad things about living on a houseboat. Actually, Honeysuckle had kept an incontinent white mouse for a while but she had to admit that having something that ponged even the tiniest bit in such a confined space wasn't a good idea. Besides, everyone knows that a dog is the only real pet to have unless, of course, you are a cat person, which Honeysuckle wasn't. There was no way that Rita would allow Honeysuckle to have a dog, not even a rat-sized dog like a chihuahua. So what could this picture of a dog in the bottom of her teacup possibly mean?

Chapter Two

Honeysuckle considered consulting the crystal ball that Lenny had left her about the meaning of the dog in her teacup.

She kept the mysterious shiny globe in one of the drawers under her lacy-covered bunk bed. The ball was wrapped in a piece of royal blue embroidered velvet and had its own small wooden stand to stop it rolling around while she peered into its secret depths. If she were absolutely honest, Honeysuckle would have had to admit that, as yet, she had seen nothing more than the smudge of her own thumbprint in the crystal ball. However, she was certain that one day it would show her the answers to mysteries as yet unsolved and the images of secrets as yet untold . . .

The boat began to rock before Honeysuckle had made a decision about the crystal ball. She could hear the slap of two pairs of trainers walking across the little wooden bridge that joined The Patchwork Snail to dry land. There was a knock on the hatch above Honeysuckle's bunk and it slid back to reveal two smiling faces.

'We could hear you singing "Super Trouper" halfway down the road!' said the face that was surrounded by a shaggy mane of tangled dark blond hair.

'You have to admit that you need us for the harmonies,' said the other face. 'Can we come in?'

The faces disappeared and a pair of turquoise-coloured trainers came stamping down the tiny steps into Honeysuckle's cabin. These were followed by a pair of long dungaree-covered legs and finally the smiley face of Jaime.

'I didn't know I was singing,' said Honeysuckle after she had given the first of her two best girl friends a big hug.

'You sing Abba songs in your sleep – didn't you know?' asked Anita (which should have been pronounced *Ar*nita but seldom was) who had followed Jaime down the steps.

'You're such a fibber!' said Honeysuckle as she hugged her other friend. 'Ooh! You're all damp! Have you been training already?'

'Yup, fifty lengths – front crawl, back crawl and butterfly,' replied Anita. She smoothed the damp tendrils of her auburn hair back into the tight bun at the back of her head before bouncing down on to Honeysuckle's bunk.

'So, what are you doing?' asked Jaime.

Honeysuckle looked at her friend and thought for the zillionth time that if only Jaime would brush her hair properly and let Honeysuckle pick out some cool clothes for her she would be so totally gorgeous. But Jaime was just not interested. While Honeysuckle could spend hours working out which sparkly bracelet looked best with which customised T-shirt, Jaime would rather be out playing football with her friend Billy, or climbing a tree or badger-watching in the local woods.

'I was wondering what the tea-leaf dog in my teacup means,' said Honeysuckle dragging her attention away from the makeover possibilities of her friend.

'Let's see!' squealed Anita, jumping up too fast and hitting her head on the handle of the orange flowery cupboard above Honeysuckle's bunk. 'Ow!'

'You've got to remember not to jump around in here,' said Honeysuckle rubbing her friend's head. 'You know there isn't room! You have to tiptoe like a ballerina . . .' – here Honeysuckle did her impression of a ballerina tip-toeing elegantly around her tiny cabin – '. . . not bounce about like a puppy!'

'Speaking of which, where's this teacup then?' asked Jaime.

Honeysuckle manoeuvred herself around her two

friends and found her pink teacup in the sink of the galley kitchen.

'Come through here – there's more room and I'll show you my mysterious sign . . .'

Honeysuckle liked to play up the magical side of her Romany roots. She would have worn rings in her ears and an embroidered shawl with silver coins jangling along the edges if Rita had let her. But Rita would rather not be reminded of anything to do with Honeysuckle's dad so Honeysuckle had to keep her fortune-telling powers a bit of a secret between herself and her friends.

Anita and Jaime settled themselves on to the velvet bunk that ran along the wall next to the galley kitchen. Honeysuckle wondered fleetingly what other people made of the way she and her mum lived. No one else that she knew had to think about where on earth to put every tiny little thing that they owned. No one else had to hang anything with a handle from hooks on the walls or ceiling – there were cups, jugs, mugs, teapots, and watering cans all swinging gently with the movement of the water. No one else's mum had her necklaces strung like bead curtains across the windows, or her collection of fifties stiletto shoes dangling by their heels from the curtain rails because there was nowhere else to put them. No one else she knew had to pack up any clothes that they were not going to wear during the following week and store them in a hut outside their home. No one else had what Rita called an 'ice cream tub', which was a bath you had to sit up straight in because there was not enough space for a full-length tub. There was no one else that Honeysuckle knew who had vividly-coloured roses and jungle-sized plants painted all over the walls of their home to cover up yet another patch in the woodwork. And there was definitely no one else whose mum did the ironing by putting her clothes under her mattress and then lying on them to get the creases out.

'Here it is, you see?' Honeysuckle knelt on the floor by the velvet-covered seat and showed the others her tea-leaf 'sign'. 'OK, so it looks like nothing that way round, but wait till you see . . .' She turned the cup and said 'Look! It's a dog, isn't it? Absolutely and completely positively *a dog*!'

Both Jaime and Anita put their heads on one side and screwed up their eyes a little. 'Mmmm,' said Jaime, 'it's got four legs all right and it doesn't look like a horse . . . or a cow because it hasn't got a dangly udder . . . I think you're right! It must be a dog! What does it mean?'

'Well . . .' said Honeysuckle, all excited, 'it means . . .' she continued before realising that she hadn't a clue what it meant. 'I don't know . . . what do you think?'

'Perhaps it means that your mum is finally going to let you have a dog of your own,' suggested Anita.

'No way!' said Honeysuckle. 'Mum would only let me have a dog if we lived in a regular house with a proper garden and that's just not about to happen.' Suddenly she had an idea. 'Maybe one of you is going to be in terrible danger, left dangling by your ankles over a terrifying precipice and the only thing that can possibly reach you is a dog!' she said gleefully. 'There you are, gripping on with your toes for all you are worth while people stand by helpless, watching from a nearby cliff when suddenly, "Woof"...'

'WOOF?!' squealed Jaime and Anita in chorus. 'What do you mean, "Woof"?'

'There's this dog ...' Honeysuckle carried on, '... a brave, black, wet-nosed dog with a shaggy tail and a face like Orlando Bloom ...'

'WHAT?!' The others giggled so much that Anita slithered off the seat and joined Honeysuckle on the floor.

'Yes!' Honeysuckle went on regardless. 'This dog has the face of an angel ...'

'I thought you said he looked like Orlando Bloom?' spluttered Jaime.

'He does! He has the face of an angel that looks like Orlando Bloom and he comes bounding across the rugged terrain just in time to catch your toe as you begin to slide towards your doom ... and he pulls ... and he strains . . . and finally this brave and noble creature drags you back to safety! There you are!' said Honeysuckle triumphantly. 'That's why there is a dog in the teacup! Oh, and incidentally all the people on the opposite cliff are singing "Waterloo" as they watch you slipping . . .'

'Well, that's all right then!' gasped Anita. 'As long as someone is singing an Abba song why would either of us worry about being in mortal danger?' She wiped a laughter tear away before adding, 'So what do you really think it means?'

'Haven't a clue,' said Honeysuckle. She looked at Anita.

'Me neither,' she said. 'Unless there is a dog outside that we haven't noticed and who might be lost . . .'

The three girls arranged themselves on the seat, kneeling with their noses against the boat's window. There were a few drops of rain clinging to the outside of the glass and the girls peered through the raindrops, which made the world outside strangely distorted. But even when they looked through a clear patch of glass without raindrops, there quite obviously wasn't a dog anywhere. All they could see was the little patch of grass that Rita called her 'landscaped garden' with its brightly painted pots, its one chubby gnome (given to Rita by a grateful client) and the bright blue hut which housed all the things that the Lovelaces couldn't fit into the boat.

Beyond that there was the road, also without a dog, and then the row of terraced houses, one of which belonged to Mrs Whitely-Grub.

Hmm, thought Honeysuckle to herself. Mrs Whitely-Grub has a dog . . . and Mum is always complaining that she brings it to the salon with her . . . she is going to have her hair done today . . . I wonder . . .

Chapter Three

'Shall we go and see my mum at work?' she asked the others when they were absolutely certain that there wasn't a single dog within sight, let alone one who might need rescuing.

'Yeah!' Jaime and Anita replied.

'It's wicked in your mum's salon!' said Anita. 'I love it when that guy she works with – what's his name again?'

'Nev,' said Honeysuckle.

'Yes, that's it! I love it when Nev has one of his tantrums and your mum has to try and hide him somewhere so that he doesn't upset the customers! Do you remember last time we went and your mum had to shut him in the broom cupboard and promise to let him dye her hair red before he would calm down? He said he never got to do anything exciting and he was wasted in this town . . . Did your mum really let him do it?'

'Mmm,' said Honeysuckle. 'She had to – he threatened to walk out unless she did. Actually it looks really good but now he says he wants to do purple "tips" as well – he's blackmailing her really.'

'Or purple-tip-mailing her!' said Jaime, giggling.

The others groaned and then did their best to leave everything 'shipshape' before locking up the hatch of The Patchwork Snail and setting off to the Curl Up and Dye salon.

The rain earlier in the day had left the air smelling damp and mossy and there was a delicious tang of wood smoke coming from somewhere. The leaves had turned incredible colours – tangerine and crimson – and they glowed against the steel grey sky.

The girls knew that they were very lucky to live in a small country town where they could walk to all the places they most wanted to go. Nearly all the people in the town knew each other and it would never have occurred to Rita to worry about Honeysuckle walking on her own to her friends' houses or to school or to the shops. Ever since she was quite little Honeysuckle had been very independent. She had needed to be. Rita had always worked at the salon and apart from spending time with some friendly neighbours when she was really tiny, Honeysuckle had, pretty much, done her own thing. And, of course, because they had always lived on The

Patchwork Snail, Rita had taught Honeysuckle to swim almost before she could walk.

'Keep your eyes peeled for my tea-leaf dog,' she said as the three friends linked arms and swung happily into the first verse of 'Thank You for the Music'.

While they sang, Honeysuckle looked anxiously round for a dog, any dog – she had to discover the meaning of the picture in the tea-leaves. She knew that sometimes she got the signs wrong but there had been lots and lots of times when her predictions were sort of, almost, practically, absolutely *right*. There was the time that she saw a foot in the tea-leaves and before the day was out Rita had dropped one of her favourite shoes over the side of the boat, into the water. And the time when there was quite clearly the letter 'A' at the bottom of the cup, that day at school Honeysuckle had got her best mark ever for maths. And then there was the time that there was just a big black blob at the bottom of the cup and Rita had been really grumpy all day because she had just given up smoking. The tea-leaves had told her that all these things were going to happen and now the tea-leaves had predicted *something* about a dog.

Before the girls got to the third chorus of 'Thank You for the Music', they bumped into Billy.

'Wotcha Abba fans!' he said, making a high five. 'Wotya doin'?'

Billy was in the same year as the girls at the comprehensive down the road but in a different class. He was quite good-looking in a tall, gangly sort of way. He had brown eyes and shaggy brown hair that flopped over his forehead. He smiled a lot which made him look nice but his nose was just a bit too big for him to be truly handsome. As boys went, Honeysuckle had to admit that he was not so bad. He and Jaime had been mates for ever. They hung out together and he was the reason that Jaime loved football and Westerns and climbing things. He was her friend who was a boy – not a boyfriend – no way, not ever, no how!

'Do you want to come to my mum's salon with us?' asked Honeysuckle.

'Nope!' said Billy. 'Gotta play some footy – d'you wanna come, Jaime?'

'No thanks,' replied Jaime. 'We're trying to work out the mystery of the dog in the teacup!'

Billy didn't look even faintly surprised about this – all Honeysuckle's friends knew about her fortune-telling obsession. Instead he just said 'Cool!' before joining the girls for long enough to sing the low harmony bit of the next chorus. This was another reason why Honeysuckle thought Billy was all right – he was quite good at doing the Abba harmonies and the drum rolls, which she had decided was a noise that only boys can do properly. This meant that there was some point to Billy. Which was way more than could be said for most boys.

Billy left the girls at the end of the song and they carried on without him to the Curl Up and Dye salon with not a single dog in sight.

As soon as Honeysuckle opened the glass door of the salon and pushed aside the glittering-bead curtain she knew that this was one of Rita's manic days.

A manic day happened when *someone* (usually Dotty, the receptionist) had overbooked both stylists. The trouble was that Rita couldn't bear to send anyone away without making them look as good as she possibly could. Consequently on a manic day like this Rita had to curl and twirl, backcomb and bleach, shampoo and set, perm and straighten in double quick time.

'Hello, girls!' said Dotty in a dreamy voice before blowing on her newly-painted Vibrant Violet thumbnail. 'Is it time to close the shop already? Is that why you're here?'

'Er, no,' said Honeysuckle. 'It's only half past eleven.'

'Ooooh is it?' sighed Dotty. 'Feels like I've been here for ever . . . If you're looking for your mum, she's over there . . .'

Rita was so busy that for a few minutes she didn't notice that the girls were there. Honeysuckle watched her

21

mum spin round the salon in a whirl of bright colours and sparkly earrings. One minute Rita was holding the dryer like a lethal weapon, twirling someone's hair around a silver hairbrush, the next she was checking to see if Mrs Gormley's perm had taken, then it was out with the scissors for a snip around someone else's split ends. Nev looked very sulky as if he might be about to threaten to leave again. Honeysuckle could see that her mum knew he was cross because she kept giving him her hugest smile and making thumbs up signals at him.

Suddenly Rita saw them. She flew across the salon and gave them each a smacking kiss. 'Girls,' she gasped in a throaty whisper, 'tell me one of you has smuggled in a ciggy! I swear by all that's pink and sparkly that if I don't have a cig NOW I'll explode into a shower of fairy dust and then where will we be?' She started frisking and tickling them each in turn. 'Come on, give it up, I know one of you is hiding one somewhere . . .' She was laughing and the girls were all giggling hopelessly. 'It's no good giggling,' Rita said folding her arms, tapping her foot and trying to look serious. She gathered the girls around her. 'This is no laughing matter – I haven't even got time to breathe, let alone talk to you lot – just look at this place! There are enough people in here to fill a ballroom and they all want to be transformed into something like Cinderella after the fairy godmother has been. It's hopeless, of course, I mean some of them are in their *nineties . . .*' she hissed, looking round to make sure that none of her clients could hear. 'And to cap it all,' she continued, 'Mrs Whitely-Grub has brought that wretched dog with her again! Honestly, what does she think this is? Crufts? I'm not running a kennel here. But it's no use telling her, she insists that the little mutt can't be left on his own.'

At this point Honeysuckle tuned out of her mum's conversation and turned her attention to Mrs Whitely-Grub. There she was, sitting on one of the pink leatherette salon chairs reading *Closer* magazine while her blue rinse developed. And next to her, on a matching chair but with his own leopard-print cushion sat her pinky-white poodle with his snooty little nose in the air, and the curls on the top of his head gathered into a pink satin bow.

As Honeysuckle stared at him a Brilliant Idea began to form in her mind. She straightened her shoulders, cleared her throat and leaving the others still listening to Rita's helter-skelter conversation, Honeysuckle Lovelace moved purposefully across the salon.

Chapter Four

'You're very quiet,' said Anita as the three girls walked back through the town, where lights from the shop windows twinkled through the midday gloom.

'I'm thinking,' said Honeysuckle.

'What about?' asked Jaime.

'Dogs,' replied Honeysuckle. 'I'm thinking that the dog in the tea-leaves was a sign to tell me that I was about to have this Brilliant Idea . . . Wait a sec, I'm still thinking . . . Mum's given me some money so let's go and have a milkshake at the Moo Bar and I'll tell you all about it.'

Honeysuckle didn't say another word to the others until they were all sitting round the black and white 'cow print' table with three tall pale pink milkshakes in front of them.

'So, now, *tell us*!' said Jaime as Honeysuckle took a big gulp from her glass.

'OK,' she said, 'here goes . . . You know I went to talk to Mrs Whitely-Grub while Mum was rattling on at the salon?'

The others nodded.

'Well,' continued Honeysuckle, 'I was asking her whether she would like me to take Cupid —'

'Cupid? Who's Cupid?' asked Anita.

'Cupid,' replied Honeysuckle, 'is Mrs Whitely-Grub's poodle – who just happens to be a DOG, in case you hadn't noticed! And I asked Mrs Whitely-Grub if she would like me to take Cupid out for her sometimes, particularly when she needed to go to the hairdresser.'

'And what did she say?' asked Jaime.

'She said that she would be delighted to have Cupid "go walkies" while she was having her hair done!' Honeysuckle said with a beaming smile.

'Is that your Brilliant Idea?' asked Anita looking rather disappointed. 'Is that all?'

'Well, she said she'd pay me for it! And there's more,' said Honeysuckle, grinning. 'I'm completely and absolutely positive that the message in the tea-leaves wasn't just about seeing Cupid and asking if I could walk him – the message in my teacup was telling me to start a Dog Walkers' Club!'

Jaime and Anita's eyes widened as Honeysuckle continued. 'You see the tea-leaves were giving me the perfect solution to loads of problems:

1. The fact that Mum *hates* having Cupid in the salon.
2. The fact that I would *love* to have a dog and I can't – and after all Cupid *is* a dog, of sorts.
3. The fact that Mum never has enough money to mend The Patchwork Snail properly and we could charge people for walking their dogs!'

'WE?' said the others incredulously.

'Of course!' said Honeysuckle. 'I can't be a club on my own, can I? We could do it together. That is . . .' she continued, looking a little less confident, 'that is, if you want to be in it?'

'Of COURSE we want to be in it!' said Jaime and Anita together. 'You're such a muppet Honeysuckle, continued Jaime. Why would you think we wouldn't want to be in it? When are we going to start?'

'How much are we going to charge?' asked Anita. 'How are we going to get other dogs to join? Where shall we walk?'

Their questions came thick and fast. Honeysuckle just sucked on the straw of her milkshake with her eyes sparkling but without saying a word.

Finally, when she had whooshed the last pink bubbles up the blue and white striped straw, Honeysuckle said, 'Come on! Let's go back to The Patchwork Snail and work everything out! We'll get some food on the way – we're going to need provisions.'

Safely back on board the Lovelaces' houseboat, the girls snuggled on to the faded green velvet bunk next to the galley and Honeysuckle put another log into the little wood-burning stove. They spread their provisions out on the tiny table that folded down from the opposite side of the living space and began to make plans.

'We're going to need a registration book,' said Honeysuckle. She scrabbled about in the drawer under the bunk and pulled out a lollipop-green exercise book that was spangled with metallic stars. 'This should do! Now, we need to make a client list.'

'But we've only got one client!' said Jaime.

'Well, yes, but we might as well begin as we mean to go on,' said Honeysuckle as she wrote, *CUPID*, in gold letters at the top of the first page. 'There!' she said putting a little star over the 'i' in Cupid. 'Now on this side of the page we'll write the date that we take him out, in the middle of the page we'll write where we walked him, and on the other side we'll write down what we earn.' The three girls gazed admiringly at their first entry. 'Each dog will have its own page, that is, when we get some others, and maybe we should write down how many of us take the dogs for walks because Billy might come sometimes I suppose, mightn't he?'

'That's a good idea,' said Jaime, 'then we can split the profits. Should we have badges, do you think? So that people know we are part of an official club?'

'Brilliant plan!' said Honeysuckle and she dug out some red card, a small piece of sticky-backed clear plastic left over from covering exercise books, and four safety pins. They drew circles on the card using the bottom of a glass as a guide and then cut out the circles. Each girl in turn then used the gold pen to write *Official Dog Walker* on her own circle of card. They had to outline the letters in black pen so that they showed up properly and Jaime wrote on two discs because she wanted an extra badge for Billy. When the lettering was complete they covered the discs of card with a bigger disc of plastic before taping a safety pin on to the back.

While they were making the badges the girls munched their way through the sandwiches, apples and crisps that they had bought and discussed what they would each do with all the money they were going to earn from their new venture. Honeysuckle was obviously going to give loads of the money to Rita to help keep The Patchwork Snail afloat but any that she had left over she would use to buy a pair of silver hoop earrings. She would only ever wear them when she looked in her crystal ball. Honeysuckle felt certain that if she *looked* more like a fortune-teller she would be able to see far more in its silvery centre.

Anita told them about the swimming pool she would be able to build when she had bought her parents a bigger house with a huge garden. Honeysuckle chuckled and wondered how many dogs they would need to walk before she could afford that lot. Then she looked up and, craning her neck, she could just see Mrs Whitely-Grub arriving back at her house with Cupid.

'Look!' she said to the others. 'There's our number one client!'

The others turned to look and Jaime said, 'Whitely-Grub is a very posh name . . . is she married to *Sir* Whitely-Grub or *Lord* Whitely-Grub or *His Royal Highness* Whitely-Grub?'

'Nope!' said Honeysuckle. 'She's not married to anyone *at the moment*!'

'What do you mean "at the moment"?' asked Anita, staring open mouthed at Honeysuckle.

'Well,' said Honeysuckle, when she was certain that both the girls were listening properly, 'the thing is . . .'

'Yes?' the others said, agog.

'The thing is that Mrs Whitely-Grub *was* married, first to Mr Whitely, then to Mr Grub . . .'

'So she put the two names together? That's not so unusual is it?' asked Jaime.

'. . . And they both died!' said Honeysuckle making the word 'died' sound as spooky as she possibly could. 'But not only that,' she continued, 'Mrs Whitely-Grub has had *two more* husbands since then . . . and I'm pretty certain that they both died as well!'

'Wow! Do you think she hacked them to pieces with a pickaxe?' asked Jaime, who had always had a blood-thirsty streak.

'Or perhaps she drowned them in the bath!' said Anita, who preferred to think of pools of water than pools of blood.

'Maybe it was poison in their porridge,' said Honeysuckle, 'and when their bodies were cold, Mrs Whitely-Grub and Cupid would go out into the garden and scrape and dig in the earth until they had made a hole deep enough to drop the bodies in, one after the other, over the years . . .'

'Eww!' said Anita. She'd gone a bit pale at this. She hated anything creepy but, unfortunately for her, Jaime and Honeysuckle were warming to the idea.

'Maybe she minced them up and fed them to Cupid!'

said Jaime, with her face a few centimetres away from Anita's.

Anita went paler still and Honeysuckle said, 'He'd be amazingly fat, wouldn't he?' And then they all started to giggle at the thought of straggly little Cupid polishing off not one whole man, but *four*.

'No, but seriously,' said Anita, 'what do you think happened to them all?'

'I really don't know,' said Honeysuckle. 'It's not the sort of thing you can ask people, is it?'

'Would the tea-leaves or the crystal ball be able to tell us what happened?' asked Jaime.

'No,' replied Honeysuckle, 'they can only tell you what's *going* to happen, not what *has* happened.' Honeysuckle scratched her little turned-up nose while she gazed out of The Patchwork Snail's window. 'The fate of Mrs Whitely-Grub's husbands will just have to remain a mystery.'

Chapter Five

'You would not believe the day I've had!' said Rita as she bundled herself and a big bag of supermarket shopping down through the hatch that evening. 'Nobody wanted anything simple done to their hair and Dotty was beyond dotty and got everyone booked in at the same time *and* Nev threatened to walk out *again* because he says that no one appreciates his talents,' Rita continued with her chandelier earrings swinging dangerously close to her nose. 'Oh – it's so lovely to be back!' she said, dumping the carrier bags down in the galley. 'Now, let's put the kettle on and then you can tell me all about your day, Honeybunch.'

Honeysuckle was just about to begin to tell her mum all about her new and brilliant idea when Rita said, 'Actually, hang on a bit would you, while I go and sit in that silly little ice cream tub and have what we laughingly call a bath?' And then, more to herself than to

Honeysuckle she murmured, 'While I sit and luxuriate in three and a half centimetres of tepid water I'll try to pretend that the last thing in the world that I could possibly want is a *cigarette*!' She started peeling off her tank top before stumbling into her own cabin and continuing her undressing. Rita's cabin was at the opposite end of the boat to Honeysuckle's, but as the distances were so small she was able to carry on her conversation while Honeysuckle tucked the groceries away into the minute fridge and the tiny larder cupboard above it.

'And another thing . . . that *dog*, you know, Cupid, that poodley thing that Mrs Whitely-Grub always insists on bringing in? He sat on one of the seats, which we really couldn't spare and proceeded to, to . . . well, *blow off*, not to put too fine a point on it! I mean, honestly, wretched little windy bag! I do wish she didn't always have to bring him with her!'

'I've had an idea about Cupid,' said Honeysuckle.

Rita stuck her head round her cabin door. 'What, Honeybunch?'

'I've had an idea about Cupid,' Honeysuckle repeated.

'Now don't tell me you've taken up taxidermy?' said Rita with a wicked smile.

'Mum! That's awful! Of course not!' Honeysuckle said, giggling. 'I'll tell you all about my idea when you've had your bath, OK?'

'OK,' said Rita as she scuttled through the saloon clutching her red and candy-floss-pink kimono round her.

There was a lot of sploshing and splashing going on while Honeysuckle made big mugs of hot chocolate in the galley. Rita sang, '*I'm going to wash that man right out of my hair . . .*' which meant that she was feeling better and by the time she emerged, pink and damp but with her earrings still on, Honeysuckle could see that her mum was ready to listen to her idea.

They snuggled themselves down under a multi-coloured blanket (knitted by Rita to keep her fingers busy whilst giving up smoking) and Rita put her feet up on the ledge opposite. They each took a sip of chocolate. 'Go on then,' Rita said. 'Tell me about your idea!'

Honeysuckle loved evenings with her mum, just the two of them together. The boat was warm and rocked gently and they could hear the logs in the wood-burning stove crackle. Sometimes they watched TV together but the screen was so small that Rita said it was like watching pixies on parade. She would rather read or make bread or just sit and chat.

When Honeysuckle had explained all about the Dog Walkers' Club – without saying anything about the sign in the tea-leaves – Rita grinned at her and gave her a great big hug. 'That's brilliant!' she said. 'Honeybunch you are a blooming genius! Thank goodness you got my genes in the brain department and not your dad's!' She chuckled and gave Honeysuckle another hug. This was not the moment to tell Rita that she would never have had the idea if it hadn't been for the gift of fortune-telling that she knew she got from her dad.

'So we thought we would start next Saturday —'

'Which means that "stoopid Cupid" won't have to come to the salon!' squeaked Rita.

'No, he won't! And next Saturday is the start of half-term and we can build up our client list during the holiday,' said Honeysuckle.

'Your client list! Listen to you, you little brainiac! Got it all organised, haven't you? It's blooming marvellous!' said Rita.

'But, what I've suddenly thought we could do,' Honeysuckle said excitedly, 'is to ask Mrs Whitely-Grub if we can take Cupid out tomorrow as a sort of trial run! Then we could get to know him a bit better and work out which would be the best walk to take him on.'

Rita was as excited as Honeysuckle about this plan and she started coming up with all sorts of extra ideas of her own. 'Maybe I could knit him a little coat with *Curl Up and Dye* written on the side, like a sort of walking advert . . .' She paused for a moment before roaring with laughter. 'On second thoughts, perhaps that's not the best thing to have written on the side of a dog that you're looking after. Might not give people much confidence!'

'But maybe we could advertise the club some other way?' suggested Honeysuckle.

'I could spread the word around the salon,' said Rita. 'And the laundrette – I have to go there tomorrow or we two will be all out of glamorous underwear – there are loads of possibilities . . . *but* you've got to promise me one thing, Honeybunch and that is that you won't forget that your schoolwork must always come first. Promise?' Rita put on her serious face, which didn't really go too well with the damp red hair and the dangly earrings but Honeysuckle knew that she really, really meant it.

'I promise,' said Honeysuckle. 'Cross my heart and hope to fly.'

That night, tucked into her lace-covered bunk, Honeysuckle looked sleepily through the window. She pulled back her red and white spotty curtains so that she could see the stars. They glittered in the sooty black sky and the moon was pale and whisper thin. Her eyes grew heavy as the boat rocked her soothingly and the little ripples splashed against the sides. She thought about all the things that had happened through the day, from the tea-leaves in her teacup to her mum's pride at her idea for a Dog Walkers' Club. She thought about going to see Mrs

Whitely-Grub tomorrow. She tried not to think about all Mrs Whitely-Grub's husbands and what might have happened to them. She thought instead about hanging out with Jaime and Anita and Billy and then she drifted happily off to sleep.

Chapter Six

'Yoo hoo! Loads to do! Shake a leg, sleepy head!' Rita whooshed round Honeysuckle's cabin scooping up stray socks and bunging them into her laundry bag. She leaned over Honeysuckle's pillow-creased face and planted a big kiss on her forehead. 'Today's the day – get up and play!'

Rita was so jolly that Honeysuckle knew she had been up long enough to renew her nicotine patches, find a suitable pair of earrings for a Sunday and practise her breathing exercises outside in the stern of the boat. The breathing exercises were all part of Rita's 'get healthy' plan.

'It's six days, eight hours and forty-five minutes!' she said.

'What is?' asked Honeysuckle, sleepily.

'Since my last ciggie, of course! And to celebrate I've

got us fresh French bread and strawberry jam for breakfast! So, come on Honeybunch, let's eat!'

While Honeysuckle tumbled out of her bunk and into her favourite, well-patched pink jeans and her black and white starry jumper, via the bathroom, she and Rita sang a few rousing choruses of 'Mamma Mia'. It might be true that a person couldn't have many secrets living in such a small space but at least you could carry on a conversation or sing a duet wherever you were without having to shout.

'There you are!' said Rita as Honeysuckle arrived in the saloon, scrubbed and dressed, with her wild mass of hair caught up with four giant, red, glittery butterfly clips and with her favourite pink and red bead necklace round her neck. 'You're going to need a good breakfast this morning – your first day as a dog-walking tycoon!'

'Do you think Mrs Whitely-Grub will let us take Cupid out today?' asked Honeysuckle.

'I'm positive she will – she was only telling me yesterday that she's going to have lunch with her "paramour" today!' said Rita wiping jam off her chin.

'Her what?' asked Honeysuckle.

Rita chuckled. 'Mrs Whitely-Grub has a boyfriend! "My paramour" is what she calls him! It's Major Wicks – you know, the elderly gentleman who lives in the beautiful manor house down the road. She says he gives her his prize-winning dahlias! Oh yes! She's quite a girl is our Mrs Whitely-Grub!'

'Wheezers!' said Honeysuckle. 'Do you think she's going to marry him?'

'Oh, I shouldn't think so,' replied Rita. 'Four husbands in a lifetime is probably enough for anyone. Anyway, I've got to rush, Honeybunch – it's much later than I thought. I promise we'll have breakfast together tomorrow. Good luck! I'll see you later.' So saying Rita gulped down the last of her black coffee, plonked the crockery in the sink, grabbed her mock crock shoulder bag, slung it over the shoulder of her leopard-print coat and hurtled out through the hatch dragging the laundry bag behind her. 'Make sure you leave everything shipshape,' she called as she reached the last step.

'Aye aye, Captain!' replied Honeysuckle. 'See you!'

As she set about washing up the breakfast things, Honeysuckle thought about Mrs Whitely-Grub. So, she had a *boyfriend* did she? She certainly was full of surprises . . . Four husbands already and now a boyfriend as well. It was too early for the others to come round so Honeysuckle put the kettle on for her special cup of tea. She knew that she had time to settle down and read the signs for the day ahead.

When she had drunk just enough of her tea to leave the tea-leaves safely at the bottom of the cup, she swirled

41

the cup round and turned it upside down on to her saucer and then the right way up again. 'Now . . . what does this look like?' Honeysuckle asked herself as she peered into the bottom of the cup. 'Hmmm . . .'

After turning the cup this way and that a few times and not being able to see any of the things she would have liked to have seen displayed in the tea-leaves, Honeysuckle put the cup down. She stared out of the window for a minute or two, letting the glimmer from the water dazzle her eyes. The she turned back to the teacup. Why didn't it show her walking Cupid? What did the strange, blobby shapes in her teacup mean? One of the shapes had two bits sticking out of it and the other looked more like a hole than anything else. If only she could work them out . . .

'Hiya!' said a familiar voice as Anita's feet and then her legs appeared through the hatch.

'What's happening?'

'Oh!' said Honeysuckle as she hurriedly put the cup out of sight. 'I had *another* great idea last night!' She grinned at Anita.

'What?' asked Anita.

'Well, I thought that we should have a sort of trial run, or a trial walk really – you know, go and ask Mrs Whitely-Grub if we could take Cupid out today, just so that we could all get used to each other! What do you think?'

Anita didn't say anything.

'What's the matter?' asked Honeysuckle.

'Oh, I don't know,' replied Anita. 'It's silly but, well, it's just all that stuff we were talking about, you know, about what Mrs Whitely-Grub might have done with her husbands . . .'

'Well, I don't think she'll have any *bodies* propped up by the front door even if she did bump off her four husbands, do you?' asked Honeysuckle giving Anita a squeeze.

'No, of course not!' said Anita giggling. 'I'm just being pathetic! Oh, that reminds me!' she continued. 'Jaime asked if it would be OK if Billy came round with her? His football match has been cancelled . . . do you mind?'

'No,' said Honeysuckle, 'that'll be great – we can all take Cupid out together!' As she said this Jaime and Billy arrived. Jaime put her head through the hatch while Billy climbed round the edge of the boat and grinned through the window at the two girls inside. Honeysuckle explained to the others what she was hoping to do, pinned on her club badge and left her friends on The Patchwork Snail while she went across the road to Mrs Whitely-Grub's house.

When she knocked on the bright red door she could hear Mrs Whitely-Grub inside shushing Cupid who was barking dementedly. The door opened just a crack and

Mrs Whitely-Grub's carefully made-up face appeared in the crack. When she saw who it was she opened the door wide and said, 'My dear! How delightful to see you! Shhh, Cupid darling. Naughty, naughty little boy – you mustn't jumpy wumpy at the nice girl, must you? Now, come to Mummy, there's a good boysy! Look at him, my dear! He loves you! Aaah! Isn't he the sweetest little fellow in the *world*?'

'He's lovely!' said Honeysuckle, leaning down and giving the little pinky-white dog a pat. Cupid allowed her to pat him once and then he gave her a snooty look and turned his back. Honeysuckle squinted quickly down the hall. Of course there weren't any bodies anywhere and there wasn't even so much as a strange mound in the front garden. 'I was wondering,' she went on, looking back at Mrs Whitely-Grub, 'whether you might like my friends and me to take Cupid out for a walk today – just so that we could all get used to each other – would you like that? You see, we're starting a Dog Walkers' Club.'

'My dear child,' cried Mrs Whitely-Grub, clasping her hands to her cashmere-covered chest, 'that would be too, too wonderful! Wouldn't it, Cupie darling, you handsome little man?' She leaned down to Cupid's level and Honeysuckle was horrified to see her let him lick her face. 'I'm having lunch with the Major today,' she continued, straightening up and giving Honeysuckle a little smile and a wink, 'up at The Manor House, you know, and I was just thinking that poor little Cupid was going to have rather a dull afternoon with us. Why! You could take him now if you like. Anyone can see that he would simply *adore* spending the day with his special friend Honeysuckle! What do you say?'

'Brilliant!' said Honeysuckle, glancing uncertainly at Cupid.

'Here you are then, my dear,' said the elderly lady, handing Honeysuckle the little dog's pink plastic python-skin lead. 'Shall I expect you back at . . . four o'clock? Would that suit you? You won't have any trouble with my beautiful little boy – he's as good as gold and never does *anything* naughty, do you, darling?' she said, looking at Cupid. 'Whatever you ask him to do, he will do it – just like the perfect gentleman! And of course, my dear,' she continued leaning towards Honeysuckle and lowering her voice, 'I shall be paying you by the hour, so you keep a careful note of what I owe you now, won't you?'

You bet! thought Honeysuckle, but she said, 'Of course, Mrs Whitely-Grub, we'll take great care of Cupid. See you later!'

The red door closed and Honeysuckle found herself on the other side of it, alone with Cupid. OK, she thought, this is fine . . . She gave the lead a little tug and hoped that Cupid, who was attached to the end of it, would follow her. Cupid, however, had his own ideas. He sat his embarrassing pink bottom down, on the front door step, stuck his nose in the air and refused to budge. Then he put his head on one side so that the pink bow flopped over one eye and with the other eye he fixed Honeysuckle with a glare that would frighten a lion tamer. She tugged again and said, 'Come! Come on, boy!' Cupid lifted his top lip, bared his sharp little teeth and growled. This is great, thought Honeysuckle. My first dog walking client and I can't get him to move a centimetre! The two of them glowered at each other for a moment and Honeysuckle began to panic. What if Mrs Whitely-Grub came out in an hour or two and found them both still outside her door? She said that Cupid would do whatever he was told, Honeysuckle thought to herself, but maybe he doesn't speak English ... She couldn't think how to say 'Walkies!' in any other language so there was nothing else for it – she leaned down whispering, 'Good boy ... there's a lovely boy ... here we go ...' and very carefully picked the little dog up. Cupid didn't look very pleased but at least he didn't growl, so she tucked him under her arm and walked back to The Patchwork Snail.

Chapter Seven

It didn't take Honeysuckle long to realise that her mum was absolutely right about there not being enough room on their houseboat for a dog. When she had managed to negotiate the tiny, steep steps, clutching Cupid in her arms (and when she had reassured Anita that there were definitely no bodies to be seen at Mrs Whitely-Grub's house) she put Cupid down on the floor of her cabin. But now, instead of refusing to budge he began to hurtle, like a maniac, from one end of the boat to the other. Suddenly the boat seemed to be full of dogs! Cupid was all over the place!

Honeysuckle, Anita, Jaime and Billy tried to make themselves as small as possible while Cupid rushed around. Honeysuckle shouted 'SIT!' in her fiercest voice but Cupid took absolutely no notice. Since he obviously *wasn't* going to do anything he was told she had to shut the hatch with a bang in case the poodle decided to investigate the outside of the boat as well. She was terrified that he might fall into the canal and sink to the bottom. Anita promised that she would dive in and save him, but even so . . .

'What's he doing?' asked Anita. 'Why is he rushing around like this?'

'I have no idea,' answered Honeysuckle. 'Mrs Whitely-Grub said that he would be as good as gold and do whatever he was told to do.'

At that moment Cupid got it into his head that there was a vicious something-or-other under one of the cushions on the seat in the saloon. He leaped up and started growling and barking at the cushions. Then he picked one of them up by the corner and started shaking and shaking it and growling and then dropping it and barking at it again.

'Goodness,' said Honeysuckle nervously, 'I didn't think he ever did anything much. What are we going to do?' she asked as Cupid diverted his attention to one of Rita's stiletto shoes, which was dangling above him, just out of his reach. He leaped, with all four feet off the seat and aimed for the shoe, as if he was a goalkeeper saving the crucial goal. Billy threw himself across the cabin and grabbed Cupid nanoseconds before the shoe found itself gripped in the little dog's teeth.

'Gotcha!' he said, with a big grin. The girls cheered, although, somewhere deep inside, Honeysuckle wished it was her who had caught Cupid and not Billy. 'What shall I do with him?' asked Billy, holding the dog at arm's length.

'I'll take him,' said Honeysuckle, reaching for Cupid. 'Look at him! He's exhausted!' She took the dog and the four of them stared at him. His pink tongue was lolling from his mouth and his eyes were bulging in their sockets.

'Is he having some kind of fit?' asked Anita, stepping away from the heaving bundle in Honeysuckle's arms.

'I don't think so,' said Honeysuckle. 'I think he just got overexcited with all the new smells and new things to look at.' She stroked Cupid's head soothingly, trying not to knock his pink bow off. 'There, he looks better now – I'll put him on the seat. He probably needs a rest after all that rushing around.' Honeysuckle put the dog on the bunk. He curled himself into a ball and appeared to fall instantly and deeply asleep.

The four of them tiptoed to the steps and carefully, quietly, crept up to the hatch, opened it and climbed out on to the stern of the boat. There were bench seats there and the Lovelaces kept soft, squashy cushions stored inside them. This meant that they had an extra place to sit on fine days or starry nights. This used to be where

Rita would come and smoke because smoking *inside* The Patchwork Snail would have been even more awful than having a mad poodle in there.

'Yikes!' said Billy. 'Are all the dogs in your club going to be like that one?'

'I hope not,' said Honeysuckle. 'I never thought he would go ballistic like that! I suppose it was the effect of bringing him somewhere new with people he doesn't know.'

'How long do you think he will sleep for?' asked Jaime.

'I don't know . . . do you think I should go and check on him?' asked Honeysuckle. The others agreed that it might not be a bad idea so Honeysuckle crept back down the stairs and through her cabin to the saloon.

'Eeeek!' she squealed and the others came bounding down after her. They were too late to witness what Honeysuckle saw, but when Honeysuckle walked into the saloon Cupid was wide awake and calmly lifting his leg and peeing on the side of the zebra-striped cupboard. As she screamed Cupid raced between all their legs and up the steps to the stern. Billy bounded after him and the girls were left to clear up the yucky puddle on the carpet.

It took ages to clean everything properly. The cupboard had to be washed with disinfectant and the rug had to be taken up, and the puddly bit had to be scrubbed and rinsed and then hung over the side of the boat to dry. Rita would have been *livid* if she had ever discovered what had happened – she might have tried to put Honeysuckle off the whole Dog Walkers' Club idea.

'Well!' said Honeysuckle when all the cleaning up was done and they had Cupid safely back on his python-print lead. 'I suppose we've learned one thing already today and that is . . .'

'Don't bring dogs on to the boat!' they all said together.

'I mean,' continued Honeysuckle, 'it's not as if we are ever really going to need to have the dogs at home. My idea was that we would collect them from people's homes and walk them and then take them back to their homes. I suppose we could offer to dog sit *in* the owner's home but this just went a bit wonky because Mrs Whitely-Grub was so keen for me to take Cupid there and then and I didn't really have time to think about it properly.'

'I'm not surprised that she wanted to get rid of him,' said Billy.

'Oh, I'm sure he'll be fine now,' said Honeysuckle with as much confidence as she could manage. 'He was just getting used to us, that's all.'

By now Anita, Jaime and Billy had also put their badges on and they took Cupid safely off The Patchwork Snail. They made their way down the foot-path that ran along the edge of the canal but the moment they put him on the ground Cupid had decided that he was much too grand to walk and refused to waddle a single centimetre. Honeysuckle had to pick him up again and carry him along the path. The three girls took it in turns to carry him – Billy didn't want anyone he knew to see him with such a girly dog. They sang a few verses of 'Ring Ring – why don't you give me a call?' with Billy doing the rhythm section.

Eventually Cupid agreed to walk nicely on the end of his lead and they were just getting to a really good bit in the chorus when Cupid suddenly slowed down. Honeysuckle had the lead and she absent-mindedly gave it a tug. Nothing. Cupid didn't move. Honeysuckle looked round and saw to her horror exactly why he wasn't moving. He was doing something in the middle of the path, which involved keeping perfectly still. 'AAAARGH!' she screamed.

But it was too late. The job was done and Cupid was looking mightily pleased with himself. 'What do we do now?' Honeysuckle gasped.

'Run for it?' suggested Billy.

'We can't do that. It's against the law to let a dog do THAT on the footpath! We'll have to clear it up!'

'Last one to say "poo" has to do it!' said Jaime and the other two instantly said "poo", which left Honeysuckle.

'OK,' she said. 'It's fine . . . everything's fine.' She tried to be completely grown-up about the disgustingness of the situation. 'We just need a plastic bag, that's all . . .'

'I've got this!' said Anita helpfully, pulling a Claire's Accessories bag out of her pocket.

'OK,' said Honeysuckle, gulping. 'Give the bag to me and you take Cupid . . . here.' They swapped bag for dog and Honeysuckle told the others, 'Go on – I'll catch you up!'

Now Honeysuckle Lovelace was not one to shirk her responsibilities and as she dealt with the horrible thing that Cupid had done she realised that she should have used her fortune-telling powers and read the signs that Cupid was giving her. She should have been able to see what he needed to do when he started sniffing around the path and slowing down. Instead of which, she ignored him and just look what happened.

Before she reached the others Honeysuckle made up her mind about quite a few things. One was that she really should have thought about the fact that a dog has to poo and that she must always have plastic bags in her pocket, just in case. Two was not to walk a dog on the path if it obviously needed to do 'something serious'. Three was to look out for the signs that a dog gives, which would tell her what they wanted. And four was to work out what the shape in her tea-leaves that morning had meant. It couldn't have been a sign that *this* was going to happen, could it? The more she thought about it, the more Honeysuckle wondered if the tea-leaves were trying to warn her about something.

Chapter Eight

By the time she had caught up with the others, Honeysuckle had decided that the sign in the teacup definitely had nothing whatever to do with what Cupid had just done. No, it had to have a more interesting meaning than that!

'Are you OK?' asked Anita as Honeysuckle arrived after pounding breathlessly through the woods towards them.

'Yeah! I'm OK – it took a bit of time because I had to find a bin and then I had to go all the way to the playground to the public loo to have a wash. Did Cupid give up walking again?' she asked looking at the little dog sitting grandly in Jaime's arms.

'Mmm,' said Jaime, 'perhaps he doesn't like being on the lead – shall we let him off?'

'OK,' said Honeysuckle unclipping the pink python-skin lead. 'Why don't you put him on the ground and see what happens?'

Jaime did as Honeysuckle suggested and the four of them watched as the little dog sniffed the air, looked round at them all and then bounded off through the woods. He bounced about through the deliciously crunchy, scrunchy, fallen autumn leaves. His bow wobbled about on top of his head and he gave an occasional 'Yap!' of excitement.

'He looks much happier . . . I hope he won't run away,' said Honeysuckle. 'If he does, Billy, you can run after him and catch him, can't you?'

'Yeah! No problem!' said Billy.

Now maybe Cupid had never seen a rabbit before or maybe he just had a bit of the devil in him on this bright October day, but moments later he and a rabbit met face to face. What happened next was not the rabbit's fault, in fact, no one was to blame, not even Cupid. He just did what he thought he should do.

The rabbit, scared by the sight of this pinky-white dog with its wobbly bow, scampered straight across the path and down into its nice warm burrow at the base of an oak tree. Cupid, suddenly imagining himself to be the brave and fearless Wonder Dog of some adventure movie, hurtled after it. Honeysuckle and the others shouted, 'Wait,

Cupid! Sit! Stay!' But would he do any of those things?
No, he would not!

Now, most sensible dogs would probably stop at the
opening of the burrow and bark a bit and then get bored.
But not Cupid. He decided that where the bunny went,
he should go too. He reached the hole and took a spec-
tacular dive down into it leaving only his bottom showing
at the top. Honeysuckle and the others could just hear his
muffled yaps as he tried to reach the rabbit underground.
It was Honeysuckle this time, not Billy, who made a dive
for him – and only just in time. His pom-pom tail was
about to disappear into a wonderland of warrens when
she managed to catch his back legs and very, very gently
pull him back out of the hole.

'Phew!' said Jaime. 'That was a bit of a close thing! We
could have lost him for ever down there!'

'Oh, don't!' said Honeysuckle. 'Whatever would we
have said to Mrs Whitely-Grub? And think what she
might have *done* to us. After all, she could be a *murderer*!'

'Didn't Mrs Whitely-Grub give you any hints that
Cupid might chase rabbits?' asked Jaime, swallowing
hard.

'No,' replied Honeysuckle, 'but I think it's just possible
that Mrs Whitely-Grub is keeping all sorts of secrets
from us . . .' The others stared at her; Honeysuckle shuddered at the thought and then looked down at the little

dog in her arms. 'Help!' she said. 'Look at him! He's completely covered in mud – and where's his bow gone?' The others started searching in the leaves for the bow and Billy got down on the ground and stuck his arm as far as it would go down the rabbit hole. Nothing. Cupid meanwhile looked mightily pleased with himself.

'We'll have to make him another bow and give him a bath,' said Honeysuckle. 'I can't return him like this! Mrs Whitely-Grub will never let us take him out again! Let's get him back and wash him – I hope Mum isn't home yet,' Honeysuckle added, feeling just the tiniest bit anxious. 'And I really, *really* hope that Mrs Whitely-Grub isn't home early from the Major's house and looking out of her window as we walk past! If she really bumped off all her husbands there's no telling what she might do to us!'

They all felt quite spooked by now. It was obvious that neither Mrs Whitely-Grub nor her dog were at all as they appeared to be at first sight.

They needn't have worried about being spotted. No one was around when they arrived back at The Patchwork Snail. Besides, Billy tucked Cupid under his coat when they got near the canal, just in case. He handed Cupid back to Honeysuckle and left the three girls to sort the dog out. 'Shampooing a dog is girls' stuff,' he said. 'I'm going to go and do a bit of fishing with my dad.'

Honeysuckle could see that Jaime was torn between staying with her and Anita or joining Billy. But the prospect of transforming Cupid was too much even for her to resist. She looked closely at Honeysuckle when they got into the warmth of the boat. 'Why are you smiling like that?' she asked. 'I thought you might be really upset about everything.'

'No way,' said Honeysuckle, re-clipping her hair, ready to start washing the dog. 'I'm feeling great!' Jaime and Anita exchanged glances but they could see that Honeysuckle wasn't going to say any more than that, so they didn't question her again.

They had a brilliant time washing Cupid. They put him in the ice cream tub bath and whooshed him down with warm water. They didn't use any soap because Honeysuckle was fairly certain that you shouldn't use soap on a dog. Anyway, the water got all the mud off and Cupid loved it. He behaved beautifully when the girls rubbed him dry and brushed out his fluffy, clean curls. Honeysuckle was certain that he was grinning when she found a beautiful piece of sparkly blue ribbon to tie round his topknot. His tail was wagging like anything.

'There!' she said, sitting back on her heels and admiring their handiwork. She tickled the little dog. 'You love being spoiled, don't you?' Cupid gave her hand a lick. Honeysuckle smiled and said, 'Now, what's the time?'

'Nearly four,' replied Jaime. 'I ought to be going home – are you coming Anita?'

'Don't you want to give Cupid back with me?' asked Honeysuckle. 'What shall I do with all the money we're owed?'

'No,' said Anita, 'you take Cupid back on your own. And keep the money in a special tin, then we can divide it up at half-term. Are you going to tell Mrs Whitely-Grub what a shock Cupid gave us by going down the rabbit hole?'

'It wasn't a shock,' said Honeysuckle. 'I knew it was going to happen.'

'What do you mean?' Jaime and Anita asked.

'I saw it in the tea-leaves this morning – I just couldn't work out what the shape meant. I wanted it to look like a dog but now I know that it was a rabbit! And there was the shape of a ring as well – don't you see? It was a hole! If I had just been cleverer I would have *known* that something to do with a rabbit hole was going to happen – I should never have let Cupid off his lead!'

When the others had left, Honeysuckle took Cupid back across the road. Mrs Whitely-Grub was delighted to see her little dog looking so clean and happy and she was not in the least bit cross about the bow. In fact she said she thought blue was 'more becoming for a beautiful little boy.' Honeysuckle didn't tell her about the rabbit hole or the other little 'accidents' that had happened during the day. Instead she asked Mrs Whitely-Grub if she had had a nice time.

'Oh excellent, my dear!' she replied. 'The Major is a wonderful cook . . .' and then she added with an unnerving twinkle in her eye. 'Yes, between you and me, he could be a very useful person altogether!'

Honeysuckle didn't know how to reply to this and something about the way Mrs Whitely-Grub said 'very useful' gave her the creeps. She did her best to smile and Mrs Whitely-Grub booked Honeysuckle for the following Saturday before paying her, very generously, for the day's work. Honeysuckle leaned down to give Cupid's smart, fluffy pinky-white head a pat before saying goodbye and heading back quickly towards the canal.

Chapter Nine

During the next week at school, Honeysuckle and her friends had lots of things to do. Quite apart from schoolwork there were:

- crossing off the days until half-term;
- making posters to advertise the Dog Walkers' Club;
- filling in Cupid's details in the registration book with –
  a) where they took him on Sunday,
  b) what happened (this was to be kept a deadly secret from Mrs Whitely-Grub, obviously) and
  c) how much they were paid;
- trying to find out more about the Major and discovering that he was very, very rich;
- trying to find out more about what happened to Mrs Whitely-Grub's husbands and not getting very far;

- feeling slightly spooked by Mrs Whitely-Grub (this only applied to Anita);
- doodling dogs on all their exercise books;
- borrowing books from the library on canine care and dog obedience;
- helping Rita get through five more days without smoking (this only applied to Honeysuckle and involved lots of doughnuts, chewing gum and knitting);
- asking Rita to knit tiny dogs in gorgeous colours that Honeysuckle could put on hair clips and wear in her black curls;
- finally getting to Friday afternoon, the end of the school week and the beginning of half-term;
- being really excited when Rita came back from the salon on Friday evening and saying that she had two more clients for the girls who needed to be walked the next day.

Chapter Ten

When Saturday morning finally arrived The Patchwork Snail was buzzing with activity. Rita was in her usual mad dash to get to the salon. She had run out of nicotine patches and was chewing furiously on her special gum while trying to attach her ten-centimetre long turquoise glitter earrings and struggle into her favourite Oxfam find – a pair of blue satin ballroom dancing shoes.

'Oooh! Another Saturday!' she said. 'Still, at least I won't have to put up with Cupid in the salon, will I, Honeybunch? What a relief! Now you won't forget about Mrs Dooley's Yorkie and Mr Smith's bloodhound, will you?'

'Mum – as if!' replied Honeysuckle, grinning. She had done nothing but think about taking the three dogs out since Rita told her about them the evening before.

Honeysuckle gazed at her mum for a moment or two and then she said, 'Mum? You know Mrs Whitely-Grub . . . ?'

'Of course I know her – to the roots of her hair and back again – why?' asked Rita as she did up the zip of her tiger-stripe skirt and pulled her fluffy orange jumper down to meet it.

'It's just,' continued Honeysuckle, 'that we were *wondering* what might have happened to all her husbands . . .'

'Goodness knows!' replied Rita absent-mindedly. 'She probably chopped them up into little pieces and put them in the freezer.' She stopped talking while she slicked on some Fruity Fun lip-gloss. 'Anyway,' she went on, as if she had forgotten what they were talking about, 'I'll have to dash – I've got an eight-fifteen cut and blow dry this morning and the salon's in a state – I need to get my feather duster out before anyone arrives . . . have a great day, Honeybunch, and GOOD LUCK!' She swooped over to Honeysuckle who was making tea in the galley and gave her a huge kiss, leaving most of the Fruity Fun on Honeysuckle's cheek.

'See you later!' said Honeysuckle, rubbing her cheek while her mum scuttled off up the steps.

'Batten down the hatches and try to leave everything shipshape when you go out!' she called as her head disappeared through the hatch.

'Aye aye, Captain!' Honeysuckle called back, and then she heard the hatch bang shut. The boat rocked wildly as Rita jumped off, then it settled back into its usual gentle rocking rhythm and Honeysuckle was alone.

There was no doubt that the tea-leaves in the bottom of her favourite rosy pink cup that morning should have shown three dogs. That was what Honeysuckle would have liked to have seen, but to be perfectly honest she could only make out two dogs clearly. She didn't waste time being too worried about this though – she had important things to do!

During the week, in the breaks between lessons, the girls had made fabulous posters to advertise the Dog Walkers' Club. Honeysuckle knew, even without the help of her crystal ball, that advertising was all-important to a new business venture. She was going to put the posters up around the town. Rita had taken one for the salon; there was a little one that Honeysuckle had already put in the window of The Patchwork Snail; Anita had taken one to put on the noticeboard at the sports centre where she trained and Honeysuckle was going to take the final one to the newsagent's that morning. She was going to ask the owner to put the poster in the shop window.

With her tea drunk and the breakfast dishes washed, Honeysuckle set about making herself look business-like.

She wasn't absolutely certain how business-like she should look but she reckoned that because her mum ran a business she could do a lot worse than to look like her. She chose the denim skirt with the bright-coloured patches that Honeysuckle herself had needed to sew on after Rita had a bit of a fight with a tumble-dryer at the laundrette, red and black stripy tights, a black jumper with a big red heart stitched on the front, six red, black and silvery bracelets, eight of Rita's multicoloured knitted dogs attached to slides in her hair and a pair of flat, black dolly shoes.

None of these clothes were new when Honeysuckle got them. She and her mum trawled the charity shops in the town whenever they could. If Honeysuckle had inherited her fortune-telling powers from her dad then she had certainly inherited her mum's eye for a brilliant bargain.

It was a drizzly morning, grey and dreary. Honeysuckle put the poster carefully into one of Rita's laundry bags to keep it dry then she pulled on her yellow duffle coat and let herself out through the hatch. As she walked across their tiny garden and along the path to the road Honeysuckle had a good look at Mrs Whitely-Grub's house. It didn't look like the sort of place where you would find bodies in the deep freeze; Rita had been joking, hadn't she? The house looked just like all the others in the street, except that it had a red front door. 'Red – the colour of blood!' said Honeysuckle to herself as she walked along the road. She was giving herself the spooks so she tried humming a bit of 'Fernando' just to steady her nerves.

The newsagent's was on the corner of the high street and the girls hoped that lots of people would see their advert in the window. The shop was busy when Honeysuckle arrived and she had to wait to speak to the owner. Everyone was chatting away to each other but Honeysuckle didn't really listen. She was busy looking at the cover of *Teen Girl* magazine when the words 'Major Wicks' made her prick up her ears. The woman who owned the shop was telling another customer that Major Wicks hadn't been in to collect his newspapers for four days and that the milkman had told her that morning that he had stopped delivering milk as no one had been taking in the bottles.

Honeysuckle could feel her cheeks go pale. It was Major Wicks that Mrs Whitely-Grub went to have lunch with last Sunday! It was Mrs Whitely-Grub who might have four dead husbands chopped up into little pieces and stored in her freezer! It was Mrs Whitely-Grub whom they had to go and see that very afternoon!

By the time Honeysuckle got to talk to the newsagent she didn't feel at all business-like. In fact, she felt wobbly and a little bit sick. The owner didn't seem to notice and was happy to put the girls' poster up, so that was good. But, thought Honeysuckle, whatever has happened to Major Wicks may not be so good!

Honeysuckle had another really good look at Mrs Whitely-Grub's house as she walked back. Was that rain dripping down the red door? Or was it *blood* . . . ? 'EEEK!' she squealed as she felt a hand tapping her on the shoulder. She turned round and there . . . was Jaime!

'Whatever's the matter?' asked Jaime. 'You look like you've seen a ghost.'

'Oooh!' said Honeysuckle, breathing a huge sigh of relief. 'I was just imagining things . . . I think.'

'What do you mean "you think"?' asked Jaime peering closely at her friend.

'Well,' said Honeysuckle, 'take a look at Mrs Whitely-Grub's door and tell me what you see.' Jaime turned and looked at the door.

'I see a red front door. What else am I supposed to see?' she asked.

'Oh – nothing!' said Honeysuckle looking back at the door and seeing that it was indeed a perfectly ordinary red front door. 'But I heard something in the newsagent's,' she continued in a whisper. 'I need to tell you about it – but not here. Come on!'

As the girls turned to walk back to the boat, Anita

arrived. She had been training for the big county swimming competition the next day. Honeysuckle tried to look as normal as possible and said 'Hiya!' brightly to her friend before bundling both Jaime and Anita down through the hatch and into her cabin.

'Now,' said Jaime, 'tell me what's going on or I'll have to give you a Chinese burn!' She tried to look threatening but Honeysuckle knew she didn't mean it.

'What's happening?' asked Anita with her eyes wide.

'Well,' began Honeysuckle, trying to sound matter-of-fact and not terrify Anita too much, 'I've just been to the newsagent's and I overheard a conversation about Major Wicks – you know, Mrs Whitely-Grub's boyfriend.'

'Mrs Whitely-Grub who probably bumped off all her husbands?' asked Anita shakily.

'Mmm,' said Honeysuckle, nodding. 'It seems that Major Wicks hasn't been in to collect his newspapers for FOUR days and the milkman says that there were milk bottles collecting on his doorstep – which means . . .' Honeysuckle looked at the others. The silence in the cabin was deafening. 'Which means . . .' she continued, 'that Major Wicks is *missing*!'

Chapter Eleven

'What are we going to do?' asked Anita and she looked so close to tears that Honeysuckle decided to try and change the subject, to take Anita's mind away from the missing Major.

'Well, the first thing we've got to do,' she said briskly, 'is to fill in the next two pages of our registration book. Then we must decide where we are going to take the dogs this afternoon. We've got Cupid booked in but we need to collect the other two dogs first. There's a bit of time to kill —' Anita's eyebrows shot up at the word 'kill' so Honeysuckle started again. 'We've got a bit of time to *fill* before we need to go and meet our two new clients, so what shall we do first?'

'Why don't you make a cup of tea and then we can see if the tea-leaves will tell you where the Major is?' suggested Jaime. Even though Anita still looked worried

Honeysuckle couldn't resist the chance to see if she could predict the Major's fate. 'The tea-leaves won't tell us what has *already* happened to him but I might be able to find out where he is *now*,' she said. 'Why don't you two make some tea while I go and get the registration book?' Honeysuckle started scrabbling about under her bunk while the other two went next door to the galley kitchen and made a pot of tea.

It took a while to find the book because Honeysuckle had hidden it so carefully. She had heard that client confidentiality was very important and didn't want their book getting into the wrong hands.

By the time she came through to the saloon her cup of tea was already poured and the others were waiting breathlessly for her to drink it. This she did as fast as the hot brew would allow. Then, leaving just a little tea in the bottom of the cup, she swirled the liquid around and tipped the cup upside down on to the saucer. She lifted the cup and looked inside. Jaime and Anita held their breath and Honeysuckle looked up at them slowly.

'What's there?' asked Anita. 'What can you see?'

'Absolutely nothing!' gasped Honeysuckle. 'There is absolutely nothing in the bottom of the cup – just an empty space where the tea-leaves should be . . . this could mean . . . where Major Wicks used to be . . . there is now . . . nothing!'

Jaime interrupted her. 'How do the tea-leaves get out of the teabag anyway?'

'WHAT?' squeaked Honeysuckle. 'You didn't make this tea with *bags*, did you?' The others nodded. 'You numpties!' said Honeysuckle. 'No wonder there's nothing in the bottom of the cup! You have to make fortune-telling tea with tea-leaves not *teabags*!'

At least their mistake made all three girls laugh, a lot, and laughing made them feel much less wobbly about the whole business of the missing Major. They decided not to make tea-leaf tea and instead they got on with filling in the registration book, planning their walk and pinning on their badges ready to go and collect their clients.

'Now,' said Honeysuckle, 'we mustn't forget to take plastic bags and this poop scoop thing that Mum bought for us. Perhaps we should use some of the money we have already earned to buy dog biscuits so that we can reward the dogs if they behave well? What do you think? It did say that you should do that in one of the books we borrowed, didn't it?'

The others agreed that that was a really good idea and they decided to make a detour to the pet shop on the way to collect their first client.

Mrs Dooley lived in the centre of town. She was very small and had bright black eyes and blond and brown stripy hair, which was scooped up into what resembled a palm tree on top of her head. In fact, her little Yorkshire terrier, Hamlet, looked exactly like her. Mrs Dooley said that Hamlet was very sociable and loved meeting other dogs. Luckily he was as good as gold about leaving his mistress and was very happy to come out with the girls. Honeysuckle gave him a tiny bit of biscuit when Mrs Dooley had closed her door, just so that he would know that they were his friends.

They walked on to Mr Smith's house and knocked at the door. There was a tremendous noise coming from inside the house. Something was howling and scratching and jumping at the door. The girls backed away. Whatever was on the other side of the door didn't sound at all friendly. When Mr Smith opened it the biggest bloodhound in the world confronted the girls. They stared at the huge dog and she stared back at them.

'This is Blossom,' said Mr Smith. As soon as he said that Hamlet started snarling and barking and growling at Blossom and pulling on his lead as if he would have liked to bite her.

'I thought Mrs Dooley said Hamlet loved other dogs,' said Anita. 'It doesn't look much like it to me!'

'Oh dear!' said Honeysuckle, as Blossom whimpered and dived behind Mr Smith's legs.

76

'Steady, girl,' said Mr Smith. 'Nice and easy,' he went on, giving Blossom's ear an encouraging tickle. 'She's not as brave as she would like you to think. I think she's a bit scared of that little fellow there.' Mr Smith pointed at Hamlet. Honeysuckle wanted to giggle – it seemed so ridiculous that such a great big dog was afraid of tiny little Hamlet. But then she looked at Hamlet snarling and yapping and at poor Blossom's wrinkly face and the girls made a decision there and then: Jaime got on the phone to Billy who said he would come and help her take Blossom for a walk on her own.

'So that's why there were only two dogs in my teacup this morning!' said Honeysuckle as she and Anita and Hamlet headed back to collect Cupid. 'I should have realised! It was a sign, clear as anything, that we were only going to take two dogs out together today!'

As they got closer to Mrs Whitely-Grub's house, Anita decided that it would be best if she stayed by the gate with Hamlet, just in case he didn't get on with Cupid at first. Honeysuckle smiled at her and said, 'OK,' knowing full well that Anita was worried about what she might see through Mrs Whitely-Grub's front door.

Honeysuckle was very keen to show Anita that *she* was not concerned in the least about going up to the front door to collect Cupid. In fact her knees were trembling as she walked up the path, but she was determined that this was only because the chilly October wind was whipping round her legs. She turned round to smile at Anita before knocking on the blood-red front door.

Cupid was yapping away as usual but before Mrs Whitely-Grub opened the door, Honeysuckle could hear another noise. Something was being dragged across the floor – something heavy by the sound of it. Whatever could it be?

If she had had to wait another minute Honeysuckle might well have turned round and made a run for it but, as it was, Mrs Whitely-Grub opened the door and smiled sweetly at her.

'Hello, dear!' she said. 'We weren't expecting you quite so soon!'

What does she mean 'we'? thought Honeysuckle. Does she mean that she and the Major weren't expecting me? Has she got him in there with her? Is she holding him hostage? Or was that dragging sound I heard Mrs Whitely-Grub moving the Major's *dead body* so that I wouldn't see it? Stop it! I'm being ridiculous! She meant 'we' as in Cupid and her, stupid!

'Cupie, darling, here's your friend, Honeysuckle! Now you be a good little boy and do just as she tells you, won't you? There's Mummy's lovely boy.' Mrs Whitely-Grub looked up. 'Are you all right, dear?' she asked handing Honeysuckle Cupid's lead. 'You look a little pale.'

'Oh no, I'm fine!' replied Honeysuckle brightly. 'Alive and well!' she added as she peeked round Mrs Whitley-Grub and into her hall. She could just make out the edge of a big black trunk at the end of the corridor. 'I was wondering,' said Honeysuckle bravely, 'whether you had heard about the Major?'

'The Major?' asked Mrs Whitely-Grub smiling sweetly. 'Why, yes, dear, I've heard it said that the old chap has gone missing and nobody knows where he is!' And then she chuckled – she actually crinkled up her eyes and laughed a little laugh as if she couldn't care one little, tiny bit!

Honeysuckle looked into the pale grey eyes and shuddered. Suddenly she thought that her knees were going to give way altogether so she bent down and scooped Cupid up into her arms and started to hurry off towards Anita at the other end of the garden path.

'Goodbye, my dear,' said Mrs Whitely-Grub waving her diamond-ringed hand, for all the world as if everything was fine. 'Have a lovely walkies . . . and take great care, won't you?'

'Bye,' called Honeysuckle, bumping into Anita at the end of the path where the two girls turned to see Mrs Whitely-Grub waving her hand before gently closing her front door.

'What did she say? What happened? Was HE there?'

asked Anita all in a rush, once they felt they were safely out of earshot.

'I don't know,' said Honeysuckle, putting Cupid down on the pavement where he and Hamlet gave each other a good sniffing before apparently deciding that they would be friends. 'It was all very strange,' Honeysuckle continued, 'and the weirdest part of it all was – that she didn't seem in the least worried about the Major . . . it's almost as if she *knows* where he is!'

Chapter Twelve

Cupid and Hamlet got on very well together. Having another dog around made Cupid much less snooty and the two of them scampered happily through the woods and tried to play hide-and-seek among the oak trees. The girls didn't let either of the dogs off their leads but Cupid was too busy running around after Hamlet to bother about going down any rabbit holes anyway. By the time Honeysuckle and Anita got back to town they had to agree that the walk had been a huge success.

Honeysuckle had done her best not to let the subject of Mrs Whiteley-Grub come up in conversation and instead they talked about Anita's swimming competition the following day. When they could, Honeysuckle and Jaime usually went to watch Anita swimming and cheer her on, but tomorrow's competition was fifty miles away and the girls had no way of getting themselves there.

'I wish we could come!' said Honeysuckle. But somewhere at the back of her mind she was thinking that she would rather stay at home and watch out for any developments in the mystery of the missing Major.

'Never mind,' said Anita, who was secretly thinking that she would be glad to be away from the whole scary idea of what might have happened to Mrs Whitely-Grub's boyfriend.

The two girls had agreed to meet Jaime and Billy back at The Patchwork Snail, so all that remained to be done was to return the dogs to their owners.

'Why don't I take Hamlet back to Mrs Dooley while you take Cupid back to Mrs Whitely-Grub and I'll meet you at your boat?' suggested Anita.

'No, it's fine!' said Honeysuckle. 'I'll come with you to Mrs Dooley's and then we can go together to Mrs Whitely-Grub's house – after all there's no hurry!' Honeysuckle knew that Anita didn't want to go anywhere near Mrs Whitely-Grub's house but to be perfectly honest Honeysuckle was not that keen to go up the garden path to that red front door on her own either.

Mrs Dooley was delighted to have her happy, weary little dog home. 'I knew he would have a wonderful time!

He does so enjoy meeting other dogs,' she said as she paid the girls for two hours' work.

Honeysuckle thought about poor Blossom and realised that Hamlet's owner didn't know him very well. Mrs Dooley asked if they would take Hamlet out again the next day and said that her neighbour would also like to have her dog walked. Honeysuckle gave Hamlet a final hug and then fixed a time to collect the dogs the following day. She and Anita walked back towards the canal with Cupid. It had been such a gloomy day that the light was beginning to dwindle already even though it was only half past four.

As they got near Mrs Whitely-Grub's house the girls thought they could see a ghostly greenish glow coming from one of the downstairs windows. Anita clutched Honeysuckle's arm.

'What's that?' she hissed. 'It's not the ghost of the Major, is it?'

Honeysuckle could feel her hand shaking. She looked down at Cupid. She had read somewhere that dogs have a kind of sixth sense about ghosts; that they can see and feel things that humans can't. 'No, it's fine!' she said, trying to sound brave. 'If there was anything spooky Cupid would have sensed it and look, he's as happy as anything. Come on,' she continued, pulling Anita along with her, 'we're nearly there.'

83

By the time they got to the bottom of Mrs Whitely-Grub's garden path the girls had realised that the ghostly green glow was only the perfectly ordinary sitting-room light shining through Mrs Whitely-Grub's pale green curtains, and nothing spooky at all.

Cupid yapped as the girls took him towards the front door. Mrs Whitely-Grub must have heard him because she opened the door before they reached it.

'My dears!' she called. 'There you are! I was beginning to get worried – it's getting so dark! I wouldn't like to think of you out there in the woods at this time of day – one hears such strange stories . . .' She stopped speaking and began to peer into her handbag. Anita and Honeysuckle exchanged glances. Mrs Whitely-Grub looked up and handed Honeysuckle considerably more money than she should have for two hours of dog walking.

'There you are, my dears! With a little something extra just as a special thank you . . . it's so good to know that little Cupie is being looked after by two such responsible girls – who I know I can trust!' She smiled sweetly at them and patted her newly blue-rinsed hair. 'It's such a comfort to find people one can trust . . . isn't it?' she said again before waving the girls goodbye and closing the front door.

Anita didn't think that she had ever run as fast as she

did then back down Mrs Whitely-Grub's path. Honeysuckle wasn't far behind and they continued running until they reached the wooden bridge that crossed on to The Patchwork Snail. Jaime and Billy were already waiting there and the four of them bundled themselves down into the welcoming heart of the boat before saying anything more than 'Hi!' to each other.

They didn't waste much time discussing Billy and Jaime's walk with Blossom. She had turned out to be a lovely dog, despite her gloomy face. In fact she was so gentle and sweet that Honeysuckle thought it might be worth trying to see if she would be brave enough to meet Hamlet and Cupid again, on another day.

Honeysuckle and Anita put the money they had earned on to the fold-down table and Billy and Jaime added theirs.

'Wow! That's amazing!' said Billy piling the coins up carefully after counting them.

'Why did Mrs Whitely-Grub give you so much money?' asked Jaime.

'Was it "hush money"?' asked Billy, teasingly. 'Was she paying you to keep quiet about something?'

'For goodness sake, Honeysuckle,' squeaked Anita, 'tell them about Mrs Whitely-Grub! Tell them what she *said* . . . you know!'

'What?' asked Jaime. 'What did Mrs Whitely-Grub

say? Did you see anything? Do you think she knows any-thing about the Major?'

And then it all came pouring out. Once she had started, Honeysuckle didn't seem able to stop. She told them that Mrs Whitely-Grub had been moving something heavy before she opened the door and that she didn't seem to be in the least bit worried about where the Major might be.

'And you think she might have been moving *a body*?' asked Jaime incredulously.

'But you say you saw a trunk?' added Billy. 'So you think the Major is in the trunk?'

'Oh – I don't know,' said Honeysuckle, 'it was just so weird that she didn't seem worried about him!'

'And what about just now when you took Cupid back? Did she say anything?' asked Jaime. 'You know, that might give us a clue?'

'All she said was that it was nice to find people she could trust,' said Honeysuckle before being interrupted by Anita.

'As if she was saying she was trusting us not to tell anyone anything!' Anita said breathlessly. 'And it was all horrible and creepy the way she said it. Honestly you can *tell* that she has done something . . . evil.'

'And she also said,' continued Honeysuckle, 'that she had heard that strange things happen in the woods!'

'In the *woods*?' repeated Billy. 'Do you think she is going to dump the Major's body in the woods?'

'Shhh!' said Honeysuckle, seeing that Anita was getting really upset. 'I think it's probably all rubbish and that there is a perfectly simple explanation.'

'Which is?' asked Jaime.

'Which is,' replied Honeysuckle, 'that I don't know yet, but I'm sure we will work it out . . . somehow.'

They were all silent for a moment, staring at each other wide-eyed. Suddenly Anita couldn't take it any more. 'I've got to go,' she said. 'I've got one more training session before tomorrow. I don't suppose either of you two is walking back towards the sports centre, are you?' She looked so frightened that Billy and Jaime immediately told her that they would walk with her.

After the girls had hugged each other and Honeysuckle had wished Anita good luck for the following day, she saw her friends out of the boat and into the gathering dusk.

'See you tomorrow!' she said to Jaime and Billy. 'We've got a new dog to take out and Hamlet wants to come.'

'And so does Blossom,' added Jaime. 'I forgot to tell you!'

'Brilliant!' said Honeysuckle, and they fixed a time to meet before the others started walking back into town.

'Bye!' Honeysuckle called again. She climbed down

the steps and back into her little cabin. She stood for a moment enjoying the cosy feeling of being safe in her own room with her brightly painted walls and her lace-covered bunk bed. She switched on the fairy lights that twinkled over the end of her bunk. She rearranged her sequined cushions and tried hard not to think about the missing Major – but her mind kept going back to the sight of that trunk and the things Mrs Whitely-Grub had said. Perhaps, thought Honeysuckle, leaning down to the drawer under her bunk, perhaps this time, the crystal ball just might give me some answers . . . !

Chapter Thirteen

Maybe that would have been the moment to bring out her crystal ball and try to discover the Major's fate, but Honeysuckle was interrupted as Rita came home from work. She clattered noisily on to the stern of the boat before arriving like a tornado at the bottom of the steps in Honeysuckle's cabin.

'Honeybunch!' she said. 'How did it go? Did the dogs behave? Where did you walk?' She plonked down her carrier bag and gave Honeysuckle a kiss. 'Tell me! Tell me now!' she said. 'Or I'll eat the whole of the chocolate cake in my bag on my own!' Honeysuckle giggled and she and her mum settled down to discuss the day.

As they chatted, with mugs of tea in their hands and slices of cake balanced on red and white checked plates on their knees, the rain began to fall. It came down in sheets, lashing against the windows of The Patchwork

Snail. For a moment Rita looked anxiously around the saloon in case any of the rain was leaking into the boat, but everything seemed to be shipshape for once. She settled back on to the seat and tucked her legs up underneath her. The glow from the wood burner cast warm shadows across their faces and made Rita's turquoise earrings glitter.

Honeysuckle told her mum all about the dogs and having to take Blossom out separately. Then she told her about the walk through the woods and how pleased Mrs Dooley was and how much money Mrs Whitely-Grub gave them.

'That was very generous of her!' said Rita. 'Mind you, she's got pots of money.'

'How come she's so rich?' asked Honeysuckle trying not to sound too eager to discover more.

'I expect her husbands left her loads of money when they, you know . . . went.' Rita said the word 'went' in a hushed voice and Honeysuckle knew that she meant 'died'.

'Wow!' said Honeysuckle and her mind raced back to the missing Major. He was very wealthy too, wasn't he? Could that be what Mrs Whitely-Grub was up to? Was that what she meant about him being 'useful'? Did she get rich men to fall in love with her and then bump them off so that they would leave her all their money?

'What are you thinking about?' asked Rita as Honeysuckle stared through the window into the black, rain-drenched night.

'Oh, nothing!' said Honeysuckle, and she changed the subject quickly. She really didn't want Rita to know what she was thinking until she had some more evidence about Mrs Whitely-Grub.

They spent the rest of the evening chatting happily. Honeysuckle entered her new clients' details into the registration book and Rita polished up the brass fittings in the galley and dusted down her shoe collection. They had baked potatoes with cheese and salad for supper and later Honeysuckle wrapped herself into her warm, soft duvet and fell into the sort of sleep that only comes when you have spent most of the day out in the fresh air.

The next morning Honeysuckle was amazed to find that she had slept until nine thirty! Rita was already up and dressed but even from the other end of the boat Honeysuckle knew that her mum was cranky that morning.

When Honeysuckle peeped round into the saloon, Rita was dressed from head to toe in purple and was sucking furiously on her white plastic 'cigarette'.

'There you are!' she said without taking the tube out of her mouth. 'I've got to go in a minute – I need to do a supermarket shop and drop in on the salon and sort out the muddle that Dotty's made of next week's appointments. Will you be OK?'

Honeysuckle nodded.

'I don't like leaving you on your own on a Sunday but there never seem to be enough days in the week to do everything . . . And look!' she said, pointing to an ominous dark patch on the ceiling. 'This blooming old crate is leaking *again* – I thought it was all right but now I'll have to see if I can get something to patch that up with. Are you sure you'll be OK?'

'Don't worry, Mum!' said Honeysuckle as soothingly as she could. 'You know I'm always fine on my own and anyway the others are coming over a bit later and then we've got dogs to walk and . . . all sorts of things to do!'

'Oooh!' said Rita finally removing the plastic ciggie from her mouth. 'You are my little star! You know that, don't you? Your old mum is just a bit down in the deadly, dreary dumps this morning but it's nothing that three hundred nicotine patches and a prize-winning lottery ticket won't fix! There are muffins for your breakfast,' she said struggling into her shiny, silver, plastic raincoat. 'Have a lovely day, Honeybunch, see you later! And don't forget – leave everything shipshape!'

'Aye aye, Captain!' replied Honeysuckle, and Rita was gone, like a puff of smoke from a genie's lamp.

* * *

Honeysuckle had sung along to eight of Abba's greatest hits before Jaime and Billy arrived. She was washed and dressed in her red cord skirt with a bright green belt, her red, green and yellow striped jersey, her woolly yellow tights with flowers printed on them and a pair of red ankle boots that Rita had found in Oxfam the week before. Honeysuckle had added an assortment of painted wooden bangles, which made a wonderful sound when they clanked together. Then she had tied her hair up with the piece of red satin ribbon that had been round the box that held last night's chocolate cake. She had been so busy deciding what to wear and trying to put her huge collection of hair bobbles and bands and bows and spangles back into their very small drawer that she hadn't given the missing Major much thought.

'Hiya!' said Jaime as she arrived down the steps. Billy followed and they both stood and looked at Honeysuckle. 'So?' asked Jaime.

'So what?' said Honeysuckle.

'So what's been going on across the road? At the – you know – House of Horrors!' asked Billy making a menacing face. 'We could hear screams as we came past . . .'

'Shut up, Billy!' said Jaime. 'We couldn't hear anything but we wondered if you had seen something creepy going on.'

Honeysuckle had to explain that she hadn't been

awake for very long and that she couldn't even think about the missing Major while her mum was around.

'Last night though,' she said, 'I did think I might try looking in my crystal ball to see if it would tell me anything . . .'

'You've gotta do that!' shouted Billy.

'Of course! You must, Honeysuckle – we have to find out what's happening, don't we?' said Jaime. 'Have you done the tea-leaf thing yet? Shall I make some tea? I promise I'll use tea-leaves this time!'

'OK!' said Honeysuckle, feeling excited about what they might find out but a little scared at the same time. 'It's lucky in a way that Anita isn't here, this might spook her out too much!' she said.

She rummaged through the drawer under her bunk and brought out the velvet-covered globe. She took it through into the saloon and set it down on the little table.

'I'll do the tea-leaves first,' she said and Jaime handed her a freshly-poured cup of tea. The others waited expectantly while she sipped her tea and then she was ready to examine the tea-leaves. She swirled the cup and then tipped it up on to the saucer. She held her breath and looked into the bottom of the cup.

'Oh!' she said.

'*What?*' asked the others.

'It looks . . .' she went on slowly.

'*Yes?*' said Jaime and Billy, leaning over each of her shoulders and trying to see what Honeysuckle could see.

'It looks like a *battlefield*!' breathed Honeysuckle. 'Look! There's this terrible angry sort of muddle in the cup. See?' She showed Jaime and Billy in turn what she could see.

'Oh!' said Jaime. 'That looks scary! Are you sure that it's a battlefield?'

'I think so,' Honeysuckle replied.

'Why would it show a battlefield?' asked Billy.

'People *die* on battlefields, don't they?' said Jaime. 'It could mean that something violent and dreadful has happened to the Major!'

'Look in the crystal ball!' said Billy. 'That might explain a bit more.'

Honeysuckle uncovered the crystal ball and she looked deep into its glassy centre, hoping, hoping that she would see something. 'Hey!' she said suddenly.

'What is it?' asked Jaime.

'Oh! It's gone!' said Honeysuckle, peering more closely into the ball.

'What was it?' asked Billy. 'Was it a dagger, or a gun – what?'

'It was a star!' said Honeysuckle. 'Just for a moment I was certain I saw a star!'

'Like – in heaven?' said Jaime, staring at Honeysuckle.

'Mmmm!' said Honeysuckle. 'Like in heaven . . .' She looked at Jaime and Billy. 'So,' she said carefully, 'we've got something violent, like a battle —'

'Or a murder!' added Jaime.

'And a star, that could represent heaven. I think this can only mean one thing,' she went on, staring at her friends. 'We already knew that the Major was missing; now it looks as though he's been violently killed – that's the battlefield – and he's gone to heaven – that's the star!'

'Ugh!' said Jaime, looking through the window to Mrs Whitely-Grub's house and shuddering. 'How horrible!'

Chapter Fourteen

'Of course we might be wrong,' Honeysuckle reasoned when she had packed away the crystal ball.

'I bet we're not,' said Billy.

'What we need,' said Jaime, chewing a strand of her tangly hair, 'is more *evidence*. We need to *see* Mrs Whitely-Grub actually doing the sort of things that murderers do!'

'How are we going to do that?' asked Honeysuckle. 'We can't stand around outside her house all day and watch her, can we?'

'We could put her under surveillance,' said Billy. 'Do a sort of "stake-out".'

'What do you mean?' asked the two girls together.

Billy explained that he thought they could either hide out, well camouflaged, somewhere near Mrs Whitely-Grub's house and watch everything that she did. Or he thought it would be fantastic if they could plant some bugs and cameras in her house. 'We would need one of those vans that the police on TV have – you know, with screens and receivers so that we could see and listen in to everything she does. We could tap her phone and everything.'

He was getting excited now and Honeysuckle thought it might be mean to point out that they could never get hold of that kind of spy stuff. 'We're not even taking Cupid out today so I don't see how we are going to get into her house to bug it. Anyway, don't you think that might be a bit complicated? I mean we can actually *see* her house from here – well, most of it anyway.'

'That's true,' said Jaime pressing her nose to the window of the saloon. 'It's not very clear though, is it?'

'I know what we could do!' squeaked Honeysuckle as another Brilliant Idea hit her. 'We could go and collect the other dogs, make sure they have done, you know, what dogs need to do and give them a quick run in the woods, and then we could walk back past Mrs Whitely-Grub's house, one at a time, over and over again so that between us we don't miss *anything*!'

'That sounds brilliant!' said Jaime. 'We can walk round and round the block of houses where Mrs Whitely-Grub lives, sort of spaced out, so that there's always one of us actually in front of her house *all the time*! How clever is that?'

Billy looked a bit disappointed that they were not going to do his surveillance idea but he soon cheered up when the girls told him that he could take Blossom because she was the biggest of the dogs. Honeysuckle told him that he was the only one strong enough to control her and that he could easily train her to be brave enough to pin Mrs Whitely-Grub to the ground should she try to make a run for it.

'Let's go then!' Billy said pounding up the steps to the hatch. 'No time to lose!'

Honeysuckle caught up with Billy and pinned on his official badge. Then she made sure that they all had plenty of plastic bags and dog biscuits in their pockets. They collected the poop scoop from the garden on the way through to the road.

They couldn't see anything interesting at all as they passed Mrs Whitely-Grub's house on their way to collect the three dogs that they were walking that day. Her green curtains were open, so she must have been awake, but everything else looked just as it did the day before when Anita and Honeysuckle dropped Cupid off. It wasn't raining though and the bright autumn sunshine made her red front door look rather cheerful, not like dripping blood at all! Honeysuckle was almost disappointed that everything looked so normal.

* * *

Things went almost exactly as they had planned. Blossom was very wobbly at first about the prospect of going out with Hamlet and Pudding, the new dog. The girls had to keep Hamlet calm by petting and chatting to him as they introduced him to Blossom. Blossom didn't want to leave her own doorstep for a while but the girls gave her plenty of time to get to know the others before setting off. Honeysuckle stroked her a lot and gave her a biscuit each time she took a step nearer to Hamlet. Then they let Hamlet walk right up to Blossom and they had a good sniff at each other. Hamlet seemed to decide that Blossom might be quite friendly after all and maybe he didn't need to try and bite her. In fact he gave her a little lick instead. Soon Blossom started to look more confident and was happy to plod along in front of the two smaller dogs.

Pudding was something like a basset hound so his rather large tummy was very close to the ground. This meant that he didn't go anywhere very fast, although his owner told them that Pudding was very energetic. It occurred to Honeysuckle that none of the owners seemed to know their dogs very well at all. Consequently the run in the woods took longer than Honeysuckle, Jaime and Billy would have liked. Pudding liked sitting down more than he enjoyed walking so Honeysuckle and Jaime had to think up games to play with him to get him to waddle about a bit. They found an old tennis ball in the bushes and finally persuaded Pudding to fetch and drop the ball, which meant that he did get some exercise. Eventually they got back to Prospect Road, where Mrs Whitely-Grub lived.

'OK,' said Honeysuckle, 'now, for our plan! We've got to space ourselves out properly. You go first with Pudding, Jaime, I'll go next with Hamlet and you come last, Billy, with Blossom as sort of back-up. OK?'

'OK,' said Jaime and Billy solemnly.

'Off you go,' said Billy to Jaime, 'and good luck!'

Honeysuckle and Billy watched as Pudding waddled off past Mrs Whitely-Grub's house. They could see Jaime looking closely at the house and straining her neck to see if she could see anything weird in the top windows. As soon as she was past, Honeysuckle set off with Hamlet. She also looked closely at the house as she passed. And then it was Billy's turn. Of course, the trouble was that Blossom had much longer legs than the tiny Yorkshire terrier and the basset hound, so Billy kept catching up with the other two. This meant that Jaime had to drag Pudding along so that she was not overtaken by Blossom, and Honeysuckle had to carry Hamlet quite a lot of the time.

Nothing interesting at all happened for at least half an hour and then, quite suddenly, something *very* interesting happened. A white van pulled up outside Mrs Whitely-Grub's house. It had *4 U 2 Hire* printed on the side and was being driven by a man in a baseball cap. Next to him was another man with dark floppy hair. Honeysuckle silently beckoned to the others as they reappeared from round the corner.

They joined her in seconds and, pointing to the van, she whispered, 'Look at that!' At that moment the driver of the van got out, slammed the door shut and walked up Mrs Whitely-Grub's garden path. 'Quick!' said Honeysuckle, 'they mustn't see us!' And she scuttled off to hide behind the low brick wall at the corner of the street. The others joined her and, making sure the dogs were out of sight, they all leaned forward so that they could see clearly what was going on at Mrs Whitely-Grub's house, hopefully without her being able to see them.

The blood-red front door opened and Mrs Whitely-Grub appeared. She smiled at the man in the baseball cap as if she knew him and then she pointed behind her to something in her hall. The man in the baseball cap whistled to his friend who got out of the van and joined him, then the two men went inside.

'What do you think they are doing?' hissed Jaime.

'I don't know,' whispered Honeysuckle, 'but it looks very suspicious to me!'

Just then Billy said, 'Shh!' as the front door opened

again and the two men came out carrying something and staggering under its weight.

'That's the black trunk I saw in her hall!' whispered Honeysuckle. 'What are they doing?'

'Taking it away, by the looks of things,' said Billy as they watched the two men struggling to lift the black trunk into the back of the van.

'She's getting rid of the body!' squeaked Jaime and the other two had to shush her before she blew their cover.

The three of them carried on watching as the two men shut the back of the van and returned to Mrs Whitely-Grub's house. The door closed behind them.

'What are we going to do?' squealed Jaime.

Billy was busy copying down the number plate. He looked up and asked, 'Do you think we should try and get the body out of the van?'

'*What?*' said Honeysuckle. 'That would be *disgusting*!' Then she went on, 'Why do you think the two men have gone inside? What do you think they are doing?'

'She's paying them,' said Billy. 'It's called *blood money* – she's paying them to get rid of the body!'

'Oooh!' said Jaime clutching her stomach. 'I think I'm going to be sick.'

'Don't do it yet!' hissed Honeysuckle. 'Look, they're coming out again!'

The three of them watched in amazed horror as the two men climbed back into the van and started up the engine. They looked at the house and there was Mrs Whitely-Grub waving happily from her doorway.

'Shall I set Blossom on to her?' asked Billy. They all turned to look at Blossom who was lying flat out on the pavement with her eyes half closed. 'Go on, Blossom – go get her!' commanded Billy, under his breath. Blossom twitched an ear but otherwise remained motionless.

'Maybe not,' said Honeysuckle. 'The horrible thing about all this is,' she said turning back towards the house, as Mrs Whiteley-Grub closed the door, 'that she doesn't even *care!*'

Jaime and Honeysuckle and Billy stared at each other. Jaime was still clutching her stomach. 'That is so grim!' she said.

They decided that the best thing to do was to return the dogs to their owners and then get back to The Patchwork Snail as quickly as possible. They needed to discuss everything they had seen in detail. They knew that they had to work out what to do next and, as Rita was probably going to be out for most of the day, Honeysuckle's home was the obvious place to do this. Besides, they all needed a cup of tea to steady their nerves and Jaime especially needed to sit down.

Chapter Fifteen

'Look, the thing is,' said Honeysuckle when the three of them were back in the little painted saloon of the boat sipping hot, sweet tea, 'that we might be jumping to conclusions.' She knew what she had seen in the tea-leaves and the crystal ball but she needed to be certain that she had read the signs correctly.

'What do you mean?' asked Billy. Jaime curled herself tightly into a ball on the velvet-covered seat and listened intently.

'What I mean is,' explained Honeysuckle, 'that if we were real detectives the first thing we would do is check out the victim's home, wouldn't we? I mean, what if the Major isn't missing at all and we've got this all wrong?'

'You don't think we have got it all wrong, do you?' asked Jaime. 'There's already so much evidence.'

'Yes, I know,' said Honeysuckle. 'There are the signs

that I read and there's the fact that the Major hasn't been to collect his newspapers and that no one is taking in the milk that the milkman delivers —'

'And then there's that stuff that you told us about Mrs Whitely-Grub and the Major being an item,' continued Billy, 'and that she isn't worried about him being missing. *And* you said that Mrs Whitely-Grub had described the Major as being "useful" which could only mean that she has bumped him off to get his money – just like she did with all her previous husbands!'

'And,' said Jaime, 'as you said, there are the signs – you know – the star and the battlefield. We *know* they mean that the Major is dead!'

'Well, yes . . .' replied Honeysuckle a little uncertainly. 'But I still think that if we are going to do this job properly we should make sure that the Major really is missing.'

'Go and investigate his home, you mean – The Manor House?' asked Jaime who was looking much less sick now and quite excited about her suggestion.

'Absolutely!' murmured Honeysuckle. 'I think we should go and look tomorrow – check it out, you know?'

'Anita will be around tomorrow,' said Jaime.

'We'd better take the dogs with us then,' suggested Billy. 'Hamlet, Pudding and Blossom's owners all want us to take their dogs out every day during half-term, don't they?'

'And Mrs Dooley said that another of her friends had

a dog that needed walking,' added Honeysuckle proudly, 'so you're thinking that it wouldn't be so scary for Anita if we took all the dogs with us to the Major's house tomorrow? Is that it?' she added trying to make it sound as if it was only for Anita's sake that any of them would need to have the dogs with them the next day. When they went to investigate the site of a possible murder . . .

When the others had left and Honeysuckle had counted up their earnings and entered all the dogs' details into the registration book, she tried to take her mind off things. She sang 'Dancing Queen' loudly with all the moves that she had seen Agnetha from Abba make on DVD. And she tried her best not to look out of the window towards Mrs Whitely-Grub's house. Although she was tempted to see what the tea-leaves in her cup might say she decided that she had already seen enough.

Luckily Rita was back quite soon after Billy and Jaime left and then Honeysuckle was too busy helping her mum mend the leak in the roof of The Patchwork Snail to think much about anything else.

As the following day was Monday and Rita had to go to work, Honeysuckle and Jaime, Billy and Anita had plenty of time to think out their plan. When they were all safely inside the boat, out of earshot of any possible murderers (i.e. Mrs Whitely-Grub) the others began to tell Anita all about the previous day's stake-out at Mrs Whitely-Grub's house.

At first Anita was reluctant to hear about the things the others had got up to the day before. She wanted to tell them how the swimming competition went, which, of course, was very interesting. She had won the freestyle race and had come second in the butterfly. This was so brilliant that they all had to have a toast and they clinked their teacups together and said 'Congratulations!' and 'Well done!' and other encouraging things before getting down to business.

When Honeysuckle felt that the time was right, she began to explain to Anita what they needed to do.

'We have to discover whether I read the signs right and whether the Major is really missing – or, dead,' she added, watching Anita carefully to make sure that she was not getting too upset.

'And then we can be fairly certain that we are not barking up the wrong tree,' Jaime said, then giggled as the others got the joke.

'So,' said Honeysuckle, trying to look serious, 'what we are going to do is to take all the dogs with us and check out The Manor House.'

'And see if we can find any clues!' added Billy.

Surprisingly, Anita just said, 'OK.'

After they had collected the four dogs and made sure that Blossom wasn't frightened of any of them, they set off in the direction of The Manor House. Honeysuckle couldn't help noticing that Anita chose to take Pudding, and suspected that this was because it meant Anita would be trailing along behind the rest of them – far enough behind to back away if they found anything terrifying.

They walked through the woods to the edge of the town where the Major's home was. When they reached the railings that surrounded the beautifully-kept garden in front of The Manor House Honeysuckle said, 'Right! Here we are. Now, we all know what we have to do, don't we?'

She looked at Jaime and Billy and gave Anita a big grin when she finally caught up with them. 'As we discussed in the woods just now,' Honeysuckle went on, 'we will walk up to the front of the house, ring the bell —'

'Why will we ring the bell?' asked Anita, who had missed this part of the plan because she was so far behind.

'To make sure that the Major is not there,' explained Jaime.

'But,' stammered Anita, 'he's DEAD! How can he come to the door?'

'That's the whole point,' said Honeysuckle. 'We have

to be certain that we really are dealing with a murder. If the Major comes to the door —'

'Which he won't,' interrupted Billy.

'If the Major comes to the door,' Honeysuckle continued, giving Billy a look that said BE QUIET, 'then we know that our investigation is over.'

'And *if* he comes to the door?' asked Anita. 'What do we do then?'

'We say that we have taken a wrong turning and don't know where we are. We ask for directions,' said Honeysuckle. 'OK?' she added.

'OK,' said Anita, gulping.

'Here goes then!' said Billy and the three girls followed him and Blossom up to the heavy, brass-studded front door. There were still a couple of full milk bottles on the step beside the door. And there were letters sticking out of the letterbox as if the postman couldn't fit any more through.

'You see,' whispered Anita. 'He's not here! Let's go!'

'Not yet!' whispered Honeysuckle and she grasped the huge, heavy knocker and banged it down, once, twice, three times. Nothing. Anita sighed and started to walk back to the front gates.

'Wait!' hissed Honeysuckle. 'We'll have to check if we can see anything through the windows! The Major might be in there – needing help – or . . .'

'Dead!' said Anita continuing to scuttle backwards, pulling Pudding behind her.

'Shh!' whispered Billy. 'I'm going to pull myself up and have a look, but I can't do it holding on to Blossom's lead. Why don't we let the dogs off so that we can look properly? They can just run round the garden if they want to, they'll be quite safe!'

'You could keep an eye on them if you would rather do that – you know, keep watch?' whispered Honeysuckle to Anita.

It was agreed that Anita should stand guard while the others had a good look in through the windows of The Manor House.

Now, everyone knows that peering in through other people's windows is not a very good idea, even if you are being a supersleuth detective; but if the members of the Dog Walkers' Club hadn't let the dogs off their leads so that they could look through the windows, the next very extraordinary thing might never have happened!

While Anita was standing watch at the front of The Manor House and Honeysuckle, Billy and Jaime were looking for clues through the windows, the smaller dogs were exploring the back of the house. It took Blossom a little while to feel brave enough to join them but when she did there was suddenly a tremendous commotion – barking, yapping and growling!

Anita was terrified and ran to the gate. The others took one look at each other and then they ran for all they were worth to see what the dogs were barking about. They reached the back of the house just in time to see a figure, dressed all in black, rush to the wall at the bottom of the garden, climb it and leap over! The smaller dogs were roaring along behind the figure, barking and barking but unable to catch up. Blossom was woofing bravely but staying close to the house. By the time Honeysuckle and the others reached the wall and looked over there was no sign of anyone.

'Wow!' gasped Billy. 'Who do you think that was?'

'I don't know,' said Honeysuckle trying to catch her breath, 'but look! Look at the house! One of the French windows is broken!'

They ran back up to the house. Honeysuckle was absolutely, positively and completely right! The French window was swinging wide open, and two panes of glass had been smashed. She didn't waste another second. Honeysuckle reached into her pocket for her phone and called the police. 'I want to report a break in,' she said.

Chapter Sixteen

'So what are we going to do now?' whispered Anita shakily. 'That might have been, you know, *the murderer.*' She shuddered at the thought and the others stared at each other as they realised that Anita could be right.

'Maybe he was the contract killer, like you see in the movies, employed by Mrs Whitely-Grub to bump off the Major,' said Jaime, her eyes like saucers.

'Yeah! But why is he here now then?' asked Billy. 'Unless the guy came back to tidy something up, because we know that what's left of the Major is in a trunk that's been whizzed off somewhere in a white van. I think I'd better go and check inside,' he said, without making a move.

'No!' whispered Honeysuckle. 'Don't do that! There might be . . .' She was about to say 'a lot of blood', but noticing how pale Anita was she changed her mind and said, '. . . evidence. We shouldn't do anything until the police arrive.'

'They're not going to think that we did it, are they?' gasped Jaime. 'Couldn't we just sort of fade away and leave the police to it? I mean, after all, we have let them know that there has been a hideous crime, isn't that enough?'

'We can't just leave!' said Honeysuckle. 'Someone might have seen us arriving – there might be *witnesses*.' She gulped. 'We'll have to wait and try to convince the police when they arrive that it was nothing to do with us.'

'But how are we going to explain why we are here?' asked Anita, who had now turned very pale green.

'We will have to come clean and tell them everything right from the start – about the missing Major and Mrs Whitely-Grub and the white van and how we came to check that everything was all right,' said Honeysuckle. She was about to add, as convincingly as she could, that she was certain the police would believe them, when the dogs pricked up their ears. Moments later Honeysuckle, Anita, Jaime and Billy could all hear sirens coming closer and closer.

'This is it!' said Honeysuckle, as the first of two patrol cars sped up the gravel drive. 'Fingers crossed.'

The police didn't seem to think for a moment that Honeysuckle and her friends and the dogs had anything at all to do with the crime. But while two of the officers were checking out the house and garden the third one, Sergeant Bootle, took down their names and addresses. It took ages for him to get all the details that he wanted and by the time he had finished Honeysuckle felt that she would burst if she didn't explain to him what she thought had happened to the Major.

Finally, turning to Honeysuckle, he said, 'So now, young lady, what exactly are you and your friends doing here?'

'Well,' said Honeysuckle with a sigh of relief. Now she could tell the sergeant *everything*. 'It all started when we realised that the Major was missing, because of the milk bottles not being taken in and his papers not being collected and things – and then we realised that someone he knew, and that we knew as well, wasn't in the least bit worried that he hadn't been heard of for days and that this person had a perfect motive for mur—'

Honeysuckle stopped. Why was Jaime digging her in the ribs? She turned round. Another car had arrived in the drive and climbing out of it was Mrs Whitely-Grub! But that wasn't all. Getting out of the driver's side of the car was a very distinguished-looking elderly gentleman whom Honeysuckle knew, using all her fortune-telling powers, simply had to be the Major.

'Oh!' said Honeysuckle.

'You were saying?' asked the sergeant.

'Um ... oh, you know ... nothing much,' she answered, while the tips of her ears began to go bright, bright pink.

Chapter Seventeen

'Well! For goodness sake!' said Rita that evening when Honeysuckle, Anita, Jaime and Billy told her all about the day's events. 'So you thought that the Major was missing because of something you overheard in the newsagent's? Is that right?'

The five of them were squished into the tiny saloon of The Patchwork Snail tucking into mugs of hot chocolate and Hob-nob biscuits. Anita and Honeysuckle and her mum were sitting on the velvet seat while Jaime and Billy sat cross-legged on the floor. It was dark outside and Rita had lit coloured-glass lanterns around the saloon; the light they cast made them all feel as if they were somewhere magical – all except Rita, that is. Rita was drumming her fingers on one of the cushions and chewing on the end of her pretend cigarette.

'Now, let me get this straight,' she said. 'Having heard that the Major was missing, as you say, you then decided, for some reason or other that I have yet to understand, that poor Mrs Whitely-Grub had *murdered* him! Did it never occur to you that the Major might have gone away and *forgotten* to cancel his papers and his milk?'

'Well, we know that's what happened now,' said Honeysuckle. She also knew that Rita was really only pretending to be cross with them. She could see little twinkles in the corners of her mum's eyes.

'But why did you think that little, teeny, tiny, elderly Mrs Whitely-Grub might have done him in?' asked Rita with her sparkly eyes wide open and the corners of her Fruity Fun-glossed mouth beginning to twitch.

'Well, partly,' began Honeysuckle, 'it was the things you said—'

'Things *I* said?' demanded Rita. The others kept deadly quiet while Honeysuckle answered her mum.

'Well, first of all you said that she had pots of money,' she said, 'and then you said that she had probably chopped up her four husbands and put them in the freezer! So we just sort of *assumed* that because the Major is very rich, she might have done the same thing to the him.'

'But I was *joking*!' wailed Rita. 'You didn't think I *meant* it did you?' And then she started to laugh – she laughed and laughed until her electric-blue mascara was streaming down her cheeks. She wiped her eyes with the sleeve of her gold Lurex hoody. 'I don't even know for sure that all Mrs Whitely-Grub's husbands *are* dead! I've never actually asked her!' Rita blew her nose on a pink flowery tissue and then she looked closely at Honeysuckle. 'So those were the only reasons that you suspected that the Major had been murdered, were they? Nothing to do with any old tea-leaf mumbo jumbo, I hope?'

Honeysuckle could feel the eyes of the others on her and her cheeks began to go pink. She was just about to confess to having read the tea-leaves (although she thought she would leave out the bit about the crystal ball) when the boat started to bounce about and there was a knock on the hatch.

Rita got up to see who was there and Honeysuckle heaved a sigh of relief. 'Don't say a word about, you-know-what,' she whispered and the others all nodded.

They heard Rita open the hatch and a voice say, 'Good evenin', ma'am!'

'Good evening, officer,' Rita replied.

The policeman continued, 'Just dropped by to let you know that the Major is extremely grateful to your daughter and her friends for disturbing the burglar and for their swift action in reporting the crime. It seems that the man in question didn't have time to get away with anything.'

Honeysuckle smiled at the others.

The policeman went on, 'I would just like to stress, however, that trespassing on other people's property is not something to be encouraged and that youngsters should never approach anyone who might be dangerous . . . but because they did such a good job, we'll let it go this time.'

'Thank you, officer!' said Rita gratefully. 'Can I offer you a cup of tea?'

'Got to get on, ma'am, I'm afraid, but thank you for the offer! Good night!' And the boat bounced about again as the officer stepped off it.

'Oh well! There we are then,' said Rita bustling back into the saloon. 'All's well that ends well!' And she gave each of them in turn a great big smacking kiss. Billy didn't look too happy about this and decided that it was time he went home. Anita and Jaime also said their goodbyes, and Honeysuckle and her mum were suddenly alone.

Rita didn't ask Honeysuckle much more about her adventure. But she told Honeysuckle again that she thought the Dog Walkers' Club was the most brilliant idea.

'You wouldn't have gone poking around at The Manor House without those dogs, would you?' she asked and

Honeysuckle promised, quite truthfully, that they certainly would not have done.

Lying in her bunk that night Honeysuckle realised how much she loved the Dog Walkers' Club and all the clients. She loved the way each of the dogs had a different character: its own special likes and dislikes. She thought that if she were absolutely honest she would have to admit that she loved Blossom best of all. Although she was such a giant of a dog, she was the gentlest and had such a sweet nature. Honeysuckle felt sure that Blossom liked her too because she managed to be much braver when Honeysuckle gave her biscuits and encouraged her.

Honeysuckle loved seeing all the dogs play together in the woods and she loved walking through the streets in the town holding on to their leads or carrying them or petting them or chatting to each one.

But her thoughts were not all happy as she snuggled under her duvet and listened to the splish, splosh of the canal water hitting the stern of the boat. There were still so many unanswered questions in her mind. If she didn't bump the Major off, what did Mrs Whitely-Grub mean about him being 'useful'? What did she actually mean about 'trusting people' if she wasn't telling Honeysuckle and the others not to say a word about what they saw at her house, i.e. the TRUNK? And what was in the *trunk*?

Wasn't there a body in there? But most of all Honeysuckle thought about the signs. What did they mean – the battlefield in the teacup and the star in the crystal ball?

Chapter Eighteen

As the day broke and the early morning light made the canal sparkle and glitter like a beautiful firework display, Honeysuckle was already awake. She hadn't slept well; there had been too much on her mind and too many unanswered questions whirling around her head. It seemed as if voices kept whispering in her ears all night, saying, 'What, where, why?' And Honeysuckle couldn't work out any of the answers.

When she heard Rita clattering about in the world's smallest bathroom, Honeysuckle made up her mind that there was only one thing for it: she had to ask Mrs Whitely-Grub for answers to her questions. She would wait until the others came round and then they could all go together and knock on Mrs Whitely-Grub's red front door.

Rita whirled around The Patchwork Snail getting

herself ready for her day at the Curl Up and Dye salon and Honeysuckle washed and dressed herself carefully. She pulled on her patched velvet jeans and her favourite black jersey. She tied the red satin ribbon round her waist and fastened it in a bow, then she pushed her feet into her red ankle boots. She felt heavy and dreamy from lack of sleep and her thick black curly hair seemed to be weighing her down.

A few minutes later Rita called, 'Leave everything shipshape,' from the steps as she hurtled out through the hatch and Honeysuckle replied, 'Aye aye, Captain,' before she put the kettle on. Then she waited for her friends to arrive. She didn't feel like reading the tea-leaves that morning. She felt wretched and disheartened for getting the signs about the Major so wrong.

'Hiya!' said Jaime as she bounded down into Honeysuckle's cabin. 'What's up with you? You look like you've been squashed by a hippopotamus! Cheer up!'

'Sorry,' said Honeysuckle. 'It's just that there seem to be so many things that I still don't understand.'

'What, about Mrs Whitely-Grub you mean?' asked Jaime.

'Exactly,' said Honeysuckle. 'Are the others here? There's something we have to do before we go and collect today's dogs.'

She and Jaime climbed out of the hatch and greeted Anita and Billy who were waiting by the blue shed.

'Hiya!' said Honeysuckle before she locked up the hatch and jumped off the boat. 'Listen!' she said as her friends gathered around her. 'We've got to go and talk to Mrs Whitely-Grub – I have to ask her some questions. Will you come with me?'

The others all agreed that of course they would go with her and they walked up the path to the road. But before any of them even had time to pluck up the courage to cross a voice shouted, 'Yoo-hoo! Honeysuckle!' And there was Mrs Whitely-Grub herself standing in the doorway of her house, waving at them with Cupid who was sitting at her feet. 'Could you spare a minute or two, my dears?' she continued. 'I've got something I want to tell you!'

'And I've got something I want to ask you!' muttered Honeysuckle as she and the others walked up Mrs Whitely-Grub's front path.

Mrs Whitely-Grub invited them all into her sitting room (where there were definitely no dead bodies) and told them that the Major had planned a treat for the Dog Walkers' Club as a thank you for reporting the break in. Then she asked them if they would like a drink. They all accepted and Honeysuckle followed Mrs Whitely-Grub into her kitchen to help. While she was in there she took the opportunity to ask some very important questions.

'What did she say?' asked Anita the minute they were all back in Rita's garden.

'Did she tell you about the trunk?' asked Jaime.

'And what about the guys who "disposed of the body"?' asked Billy.

'Tell us!' they all said together, clustering closely round Honeysuckle so as not to miss a single word.

'Well . . .' said Honeysuckle.

'Yes?' prompted Jaime.

'Well, the first thing she said was that the Major has invited us all to go to that posh restaurant in town tonight. He wants to treat us, Mum included, to a slap-up meal!' said Honeysuckle.

'Wow!' gasped the others.

'But what about the trunk?' asked Billy.

'The trunk was full of books,' began Honeysuckle. 'She was giving them to the man in the van who was her *son* and who lives with his father, Mrs Whitely-Grub's *ex-husband* who is alive and well and living in Manchester!'

'So that's one husband that she definitely didn't bump off!' said Anita looking very cheered by the whole idea.

'And,' continued Honeysuckle, 'of course the reason Mrs Whitely-Grub didn't look worried about the Major was because she *knew* he was in Scotland! And when I come to think about it she only said that she "had heard it said" that the Major was missing, she didn't say that he definitely was! That was why she smiled when she said it, because she had heard rumours that people were concerned about him but she knew he was completely safe! She said she knew it was stupid of her, but she hadn't told the newsagent or the milkman because she didn't want the Major to think that she was interfering.'

'But what about him being "useful"?' asked Billy.

'I couldn't really ask her that,' said Honeysuckle, 'but she did say that she hopes he has caught lots of salmon because he is such "a marvellous cook" – so that's probably what she meant by being "useful" – being able to cook!'

'So the bit about "trusting people" must have meant that she really does trust us to look after Cupid – not to keep secrets at all!' Jaime squealed, delighted that she had worked out this final mystery.

But then she and the others realised that there was still something that didn't make sense – the signs that Honeysuckle saw. None of them liked to ask her about her fortune-telling predictions and they made a vow between themselves not to mention the signs again.

* * *

Although the friends had a fabulous time that day walking Blossom and Hamlet and Pudding and the new client, Doris, Honeysuckle felt uneasy. The day was bright and breezy but she felt dull and a little sad. She just couldn't believe that she had misread the tea-leaves and the crystal ball. She was absolutely, totally and completely certain that she had a real fortune-telling gift, so why did she get it all so wrong?

The meal that evening was fabulous too. Honeysuckle and her mum had dressed themselves up to the nines, and even though Honeysuckle had put on every sparkly thing that she owned, including a long, glittery pink ballet skirt, silvery tights and a diamanté tiara, she still didn't feel very happy.

Right at the end of the meal, when Honeysuckle, Jaime, Billy and Anita had scraped the last of the chocolate fudge gateau off their plates, Rita turned to the Major and said, 'You must be so relieved that the burglar didn't manage to take anything!'

'Ah, well,' said the Major in his posh, gruff voice, 'unfortunately my dear, that is not the case!'

'Oh my goodness!' said Rita, and the others pricked up their ears.

The Major continued. 'No – the wretch did get away with something but I only discovered it was missing this afternoon.'

'What was it that he took?' asked Honeysuckle, feeling the hairs on the back of her neck start to prickle and send shivers down her spine.

'He took a medal. A medal that my grandfather won at a battle during the Boxer Uprising – a rather beautiful and valuable medal called the Star of India.'

Chapter Nineteen

Much later that evening, by the light of a watery moon, when Honeysuckle was certain that Rita was asleep, she gazed into the murky depths of the crystal ball.

While the water splashed gently against the sides of The Patchwork Snail, Honeysuckle smiled to herself. She knew that what she had seen at the bottom of her teacup before the discovery of the burglar was indeed a battlefield. It was the battlefield where the Major's grandfather had won his medal. The star that she thought she had seen in the crystal ball was, of course, the Star of India. She could have predicted exactly what was going to happen if only she had been able to understand the signs! Honeysuckle hugged herself – she *did* have fortune-telling powers but maybe she hadn't quite learned how to completely understand them yet.

She peered again into the crystal ball. Her eyes were getting heavy but just before she climbed into her bunk and slipped into that warm, safe place where wonderful dreams are made and Abba play non-stop, she was certain that she saw something. There, for a fleeting moment in the centre of the ball was a dark-haired girl, just like Honeysuckle herself, looking back at her. The girl was smiling happily and she was surrounded by dozens and dozens of barking, wagging dogs! The Dog Walkers' Club was going to be *very* busy.

Cherry Whytock used to be a country bumpkin but is now struggling to become a glossy girl-about-town. She spends a great deal of time in the local coffee shop, gathering strength for her next retail expedition, but becoming a sophisticated 'townie' is proving to be more difficult than she imagined. Even though she now owns at least a million pairs of high-heeled shoes she still feels happier in her wellies. If anything Lily, her boxer, is more of a glossy girl-about-town as she now has a beautiful pink sparkly collar, which she enjoys showing off to her various boyfriends on the common. (Lily has dumped the wire-haired dachshund that she used to be in love with because he kept stealing her biscuits.)

Look out for these other Piccadilly Pearls

VENUS SPRING: STUNT GIRL
by Jonny Zucker

Venus Spring is fourteen years old and this is the first summer she's been allowed to go to stunt camp. It's a dream come true; something she has been working towards for years. But while she's there she stumbles on a devious and terrifying plot that threatens the surrounding countryside.

'A fast-paced, thrilling read'
The Sunday Times

VENUS SPRING: BODY DOUBLE
by Jonny Zucker

When Venus Spring's friend, DCI Radcliff, hears rumours that a gang are going to kidnap the child star, Tatiana Fairfleet, she wants to give Tatiana some protection without causing panic. So she asks Venus to act as Tatiana's body double at her boarding school – providing a decoy if there are any problems.
Venus finds herself caught in real danger.
She must use all her skills to stop events spiralling out of control.

GIRL WRITER: CASTLES AND CATASTROPHES
by Ros Asquith

Cordelia Arbuthnott wants to write books. Not the
sort that her aunt, the bestselling children's author
Laura Hunt writes, but literary masterpieces.
But writing a masterpiece is trickier than she
expected. Real life just keeps getting in the way!
Welcome to the wacky, hilarious world of Cordelia.
And for readers who are also aspiring writers, there are
some fantastic top tips on getting your story right.

SEAGIRLS: THE CRYSTAL CITY
by g.g. elliot

Polly Jenkins had always felt different to other girls.
But then she finds a kindred spirit in Lisa, who she
meets at a swimming competition. As the two become
friends, they discover that they both have the same
fish-shaped birthmark, they were both adopted . . . and
they can both swim underwater. When a strong current
drags them deep into the sea, they are taken to a world
more incredible and more disturbing than they
could ever have imagined.

☆

www.piccadillypress.co.uk

☆ The latest news on forthcoming books

☆ Chapter previews

☆ Author biographies

☆ Fun quizzes

☆ Reader reviews

☆ Competitions and fab prizes

☆ Book features and cool downloads

☆ And much, much more . . .

Log on and check it out!

Piccadilly Press

☆